STOLEN DOVE

STOLEN HEARTS SERIES

CARINA BLAKE

ISBN: 9798709925564

Copyright © 2021 by Carina Blake

All rights reserved.

No part of this book may be reproduced in any form or by any electronic or mechanical means, including information storage and retrieval systems, without written permission from the author, except for the use of brief quotations in a book review.

PROLOGUE

Victor

"Your father has to be handled." I raise my brows, staring at my right-hand man, Fernando, waiting for him to elaborate on such a bold statement. If he was anyone else, I'd bust his face in. Besides, he does have a point.

It's merely six in the morning, and I have a fucking headache building in my temples. I roll my hand, ushering him into speaking before my temper worsens.

"He's cost us three shipments of product to the Italians. They're moving guns along with the drugs and easily stole our merchandise without consequence. Soon they'll take over, killing everyone including your family —because they know you're not going to fall in line," he finishes. My fist contracts and releases against the leather armrest of my chair, flexing as my anger amplifies.

I've only just arrived from Oxford a week ago after getting my business degree. My intentions were to continue growing my family vineyard and winery while leaving my crimes in the past, but it seems the old bastard would rather chase tail than handle the business. So, now I'm in the middle of a crumbling empire, failing both the legal and illegal sides of our businesses with the looming threat of the Italians sweeping in.

Despite having grown up on the family estate, I'm forced to use the manager's office at the winery and restaurant to get shit done because my father can't be trusted. I can't just walk away from the family like I thought I could because there are too many lives depending on me, which I'm sure is what Fernando's trying to get at.

Ten years my senior, he's my best friend and my personal guard, making sure I'm kept in the loop about as much as possible—even the fact that my father's habits have put us in a perilous situation. It's either we let the Sicilians control and wipe out my family and all those loyal to me, or we take back control. There's no fucking middle ground with these assholes.

Slamming my hands on the armrests, I bolt upright, standing in one smooth motion. I tug on my suit pants to straighten them out and adjust my suit jacket, looking like the leader I'm meant to be. I'm not a sloppy fucker like my father; my body's taut and strong and my suits are impeccably made by my tailor in London. I will command respect. There can be no other way.

"Fuck, yeah, I'm not. I'll destroy each and every one of them if they cross me. I'll deal with my father, but I need our men to be ready. We're going to run these babasos out of our country. They're too weak to take their country, so they come here to start shit. Well, I'm not having it. I'm the new head of the Serrano Family. I want a meeting with my men before we take our shit back and then some. Get the word out." I don't need this fucking shit, but as the future king of the Serrano empire, I must wrest control away from the jester on my throne.

"I'll set it up now. What about your mother and brother?" My weakness. My kryptonite. I'd do anything for them and my father knows it, which means I need to act wisely and not in haste.

"Move them into hiding. She left him last week, taking Hector with her. I'm sure he's itching to get back at her—and me for helping her escape his grips." As soon as my feet touched Spanish soil, my mother fled my father's hold for good. It's for the best, but he probably doesn't see it that way. After all, no one leaves the great Victor Serrano Jr. I am the third and last Victor Serrano. If I do have children, that name is out the window.

Fernando nods, understanding how much my family means to me. "He was hoping to get your brother to do the cocaine run last week, but you stopped that shit by coming home." That pisses me off more than anything because I asked my father to leave my brother out of it and to not get his hands dirty. I kept tabs on Hector and so far he's been clean, but it's not for my father's lack of trying, since now Hector is considered a man.

I'm almost twenty-two and have seen more shit than most men will ever see, and I don't want that for him. My little brother is supposed to go away to college now like I had and choose his path. I want him to go to college in the States, but I can't let him go unprotected while my father has made us targets. After Hector returns and should he want to follow beside me and the organization, I won't stop him. However, not until he's had a life free from this shit will I demand that of him.

"Hector's only seventeen. He doesn't need to be mixed up in that shit. I want them protected at all costs. The old man could be blown to smithereens, and I wouldn't give two fucks. He deserves his fate over and over. Whether he chooses to step down peacefully or have power snatched from him will be his choice. My loyalty has never been to him but to my mother, brother, and my ancestors who built the empire he's tearing asunder."

"I'm by your side, Victor." I pull him in for a one-armed hug and then step back. "I know I can always count on you. It's time to pay my father a visit." I pull out my gun, slide it back to empty the chamber, and unload the magazine to check it before reloading the fucker. "Do you know how many are still loyal to him?"

He shakes his head lightly in frustration. "Not many. The unrest is growing. After Benito's death and lack of retribution, the men aren't happy."

Right before I finished school, my father had them moving a shipment of stolen metal out of the Sicilians' personal cargo freighter. They were caught and bullets went flying, killing one of the family's longest, most loyal employees. No retaliation, no vindication, and then he played it off as Benito doing the heist on his own, disavowing all connection to it and essentially apologizing to the fuckers, which is why they didn't hesitate to steal our shit. His cowardice will make it easier for me to gain the loyalty and trust of my father's men.

"Understood." Tucking my gun under my suit jacket, I straighten my shoulders and say, "Vámonos."

We leave my office inside the winery, exiting the opposite direction of the restaurant area to my vehicle in the back. He clicks the unlock button and hits the remote start, causing the explosives inside it to detonate.

I don't know what comes first, but the impact of the explosion sends us flying back on our asses. A crowd of employees getting started for the day forms. I stand up, a little shaken but a hell of a lot pissed the fuck off. "Cameras, horita!" I bark as I help Fernando to his feet. He's got a cut on his face from a shard of glass or shrapnel. "Medicos," I add. I can't have my man down like that. "Take a seat. We'll get you some help. Then we're going to put bullets in their heads."

He nods, but I'm not sure he's all there. He'd been two feet in front of me and had felt the full impact, shielding me.

Two minutes later, the manager of my winery comes with the hidden surveillance cameras. We watch the footage in the security of my office to see it's my half brother Julio's buddy, who works for my father. "He's a dead man. Pull all his calls. I want them yesterday. All hush. We don't know who's the traitor, or if he came from my father or my stepbrother." Julio has been looking to replace me since the day he was born. I fucked up his plans by coming home. With me out of the way, he'll think that he takes over. He's the stupidest motherfucker because I'm deadlier than any of my father's men, and blood means shit to me. I owe no one my fealty, especially my father's leftovers.

A waitress, Marisol, brings out the first-aid case and works on Fernando's face, gently cleansing it. "Basta. I'm fine." He brushes her hand away and then stands. "I'm going with you. I want answers."

I don't argue because I'd demand the same. This won't go unanswered. Retaliation will be had. My head's still fucking spinning as we attempt to make ourselves presentable. I check my weapon, and so does Fernando. We're ready to take heads.

After checking security footage for the front of the restaurant, we head out to our other vehicle, starting it and jumping in. We barely pull out of the lot when my phone rings, and it's Hector. "Que te paso?" I answer without hesitation for him. He should be up getting ready for his last week at school.

"Mama. She's in the hospital. There was an accident," he blurts out, voice cracking.

"I'm on my way. How is she?"

"She's in surgery."

"Accident, my ass. There's a lot of shit about to go down after today."

"I'm with you."

"No. You're going to finish school and go off to college," I ordered. He might refuse me as his brother, but not as jefe.

"Enough with that bullshit."

"We'll talk about that later. I'm on my way. I need someone to look at Fernando too. Someone we trust. Sabes?" I look at Fernando who rolls his eyes, thinking that he doesn't need medical attention.

"Si." I end the call and speed like the devil is on my

shoulder. I know he's not just on my shoulder but embedded in my soul, and the war is just getting started.

"I don't need a doctor," he insists, and yet I'm the one driving because he's not sturdy enough.

"I need my best man one hundred, sabes?"

He grumbles but relents. Not like he had a fucking choice anyway.

The second I arrive at the hospital, Hector's there with Marcelino, waiting for us.

"Park it," I tell Marcelino.

He nods and looks at Fernando. "War's brewing, isn't it?"

"Yes, it is."

"Bueno."

He pulls away to the parking spots, and I hook my arm around my brother's shoulder. "Lead me to her."

"She's still in surgery, but they say she'll make it."

"She better, or more heads will roll."

"Is this the man we're supposed to look at?" A petite nurse comes up to us, cocking her brow up at Fernando with more attitude than she should have for her size. Then again, the little ones are the most feisty.

"Si, por favor."

She nods and says, "Follow me." Fernando wags his brows, eyeing her round ass. All of a sudden, he wants to be seen.

"Have you called our father?" I ask Hector while watching Fernando until he disappears out of view. I'm sure there's nothing to worry about there. Fernando can handle himself, or at least I hope so.

"Yes, but he didn't seem concerned."

I nod, looking around the room for trouble before saying, "Fuck him. He ain't gonna be shit soon."

"About time." The smirk on his face says it all. My brother has been waiting for me to return and take over—just like many of these guys.

Marcelino comes in and says, "So what's the plan? What do you need from me?"

"Loyalty."

"Without a doubt."

"Even if it means cleaning house?"

"Whatever it takes to keep from ending up like Benito." We shake hands.

Hector turns his attention to the hallway, gaining my attention as well to approaching medical staff. "How is she?" he asks.

"Señor Serrano, your mother is doing fine. She's in recovery at the moment, but she'll be able to have visitors in an hour."

"What are her injuries?" I ask.

"I'm sorry, but who are you?"

"I'm the one who you will speak to from now on. I'm her oldest son, Victor Serrano."

"Oh, my apologies, Señor Serrano. Your mother has received two broken ribs, one broken leg, and several lacerations and abrasions all over her body from the impact of the crash."

"All of them are consistent with a car crash?"

"Yes, although I do recommend you speak with the police regarding the accident itself. If you'll excuse me, I have another surgery." I nod and shake his hand.

"We're going to have a lot of business to take care of

pretty soon." I take a seat with my back to the wall so I can see all around me as I plot my next course of action.

We pull up to the gate, and the head of my father's security lets us through without asking questions. "Is my father alone?" I've already scooped up my would-be assassin, ready to interrogate and then destroy him. He'll be my first round of business when I take my rightful place as the head of the family.

"No. He has one of his special guests. Barely legal," he scoffs. Felipe has been with the family for over ten years and has witnessed the countless parade of women in the house. That ends today. The next female to enter this home that isn't staff or family will have my name.

I can't hide my disgust. I should have gotten my mother out sooner, but I couldn't protect her from a distance, and I needed to be out of my father's reach to gain the knowledge and connections that I needed to take power. "Things will be changing today. I'm looking for loyal men, Felipe. Are you planning to stop me?" I open my jacket and reveal my piece as I flick off the safety.

"No. I'm your man, Jefe." He puts his hands in front of him to show no interest in being trouble. "There are only two guards in the house, and they will not fight you. One is Benito's son." I'm surprised they haven't defected sooner.

"Bueno. Any opposition will be crushed. I don't give two fucks who gets in my way. I will do what I have to do to secure this family again."

"Including those fucks that took out Benito?" he asks as if my answer determines how far he's willing to go, which I understand, because they put their lives and loyalty in my father's hands and he betrayed them.

"I'll do my best to make them pay." I don't know how, but any crimes committed against the Serrano family, against me, will be avenged.

"That is all I need." We shake, and I drive on through to the front of the house. Stepping onto the stone path, I feel power washing over me. *I am the king.*

"Do you want me to stand guard or go with you?"

I clap my hand on his shoulder, grateful to have him as my friend. He's been loyal to me more than any person I know.

"Stand guard. I trust Felipe and maybe Benito's boy, but I don't want anyone to show up, and I want to speak to the prick alone—that way, he'll talk. If you're there, he might shut up." My father never cared for Fernando, and with good reason, too, because he stood at my side and was there for my accomplishments.

My father didn't hate me, so to speak, but he envied my youth because he refused to give up his own, partying like a young man and chasing pussy everywhere while refusing to relinquish power. That ends today.

"Good." He nods and stands just inside the front door with it wide open, ready to refuse entry to anyone.

I enter my ancestral home and go straight to my father's office, and not a soul attempts to stop me. That's good.

Where are all the staff members? Not a single guard nearby? Interesting.

A memory from my childhood hits me. It was the first time I'd found my father with another woman. I had to have only been about five when I walked into his office and there he was, banging this broad on his desk. I remember thinking he was hurting her, but then my nanny came and grabbed me, taking me back to my room and telling me that I was never to enter my father's rooms without knocking. Later that night, I had a new nanny and the old one was never seen again. It wasn't until I was sixteen that I learned my father killed her for letting me walk in on him. He was never to be interrupted again, and the staff knew it. It's never happened again, but usually there's someone standing guard to make sure.

I open his office door to find him groaning while some little bitch sits at his feet, topless and servicing him, moaning like she actually likes it.

His eyes flash open when she flops backward with her tits bouncing, his face white as a ghost from being caught unawares. God, I could have put a bullet in head; he wouldn't even have seen me. Weak old bastard, trying to hold on to his virility.

"Get the fuck out, now," I order the little puta. She climbs off her knees, and my father doesn't even bother to help her up. She stumbles as she gets her things and rushes out past me. I slam the door shut behind her, listening to the wood vibrate from the force, hoping he understands this isn't a social visit.

"Son, what are you doing here?" he asks with a shaky voice. Slowly the color returns to his face.

"So Mama is in the hospital, and you're too busy getting a blow job to go see her," I toss out. He has spent a lifetime making her life difficult for no other reason than he could. He showed no loyalty to the woman who was supposed to be his queen. He betrayed her at every turn, and I can't say that I'm surprised by his lack of concern, but I do wonder if there's more going on.

He laughs and then shrugs. "This is why you interrupted me? She left me, so why the hell should I give a fuck that she was run off the road? Frankly, they didn't do a good enough job."

"Are you telling me you set this up?" My calm tone belies the seething rage amplifying by the second. Does he have no idea how much my mother means to me? The crazy son of a bitch has just signed his death certificate while being none the wiser.

"No one makes me look stupid." Nope. He's a clueless idiot.

"Too late. You've done that shit on your own. You're weak, caving to the Sicilians just so you can get your rocks off," I practically spit out in absolute disgust, which he fucking scoffs away.

He waves his hand dismissively as if Benito's life meant nothing. "Losing one guy isn't enough to go to war with them. They've got enforcements in the States and Sicily."

"I'm surprised I didn't come in to find you taking it up the ass by one of them, you fucking coward."

"Who the fuck are you to question me?" he roars, trying to intimidate me, which is futile because this man doesn't inspire an ounce of fear in me.

"I'm the head of the Serrano family," I inform him.

He chuckles. "You'll have to pry it from my cold

hands." I've heard enough. I pull out my Sig Sauer and pop off one shot to his head. He flops down face first, hitting his desk and then bouncing to the floor with his pants still down. A smirk spreads over my face as the rush of satisfaction comes over me. He taught me how to kill and never let the enemy see weakness. Lesson learned.

Fernando rushes in, and Benito Jr. and Gustavo follow with their guns out. Seeing the scene before them, they put them away. "El rey esta muerto. ¡Larga vida al rey!" Benito Jr. shouts.

"¡Que viva el rey!" Fernando and Gustavo cheer together.

"Dispose of this wretch. I have work to do."

"With pleasure. Forever in your debt."

"Viva la Casa de Serrano!" I roar.

"Serrano!" They cheer. It's time to clean house, and I will.

"We have another visit to make." We have to finish this morning's business with my half brother's bitch-ass errand boy.

"Where the fuck is the rest of the staff?" I ask as I walk around the first floor of the house to determine how much I'm going to have to upgrade. Luckily, that prick didn't get a hold of my money or I'd have to kill him again. There are some things I can sell, but most of this shit is outdated and worthless. It'll just end up in the trash.

"Most of them left when your father refused to pay them." I've been going over the books for the winery, and it's not doing terribly. We'll need more branding and a fuckton of marketing to bring it back to how it was when

I left. My grandfather would be turning over in his grave to see his own grandparents' vineyard in its current state.

"Refused to pay them?" It's not hard to see that he's been short on funds, but where is the money going? I'm guessing the Italians.

"Yeah—the cook, the landscaper, even the new housekeeper booked it. That one in there earlier was vying for the position." The only position she was shooting for was the one on her knees.

"I want this house renovated, and I'll be doing the hiring. "Felipe, make a note of everything we need to do to this place and what staff I can hire. At this point, I'll only need a housekeeper and cook and weekly grounds work. Get me a list of viable candidates, and none like that dumb broad that just left. I'm not looking to continue the cesspool going on. We'll be back this evening to go over everything." We shake on it, and Fernando and I get back in the SUV to deal with poor, foolish Oscar.

We make it to the warehouse in record time across town as I change into a pair of disposable pants and a tee shirt. I don't need to ruin a good suit. When I slam the door open, my men smile and my enemy shrieks like a little girl. "What a greeting. Men, you can wait outside. It's about to get messy."

I stare at the little fuck who tried to kill me this morning. His feet and hands are bound as he sits in a chair, pissing himself. I need to remind myself to redo this property for proper ventilation and drainage. He's scared, and he should be because he picked a fight with Satan himself, and I don't give second chances. "So tell me, Oscar." I pause, running the dull side of my knife under my chin, prolonging this moment. I want him ready to beg before I kill him. His legs shake with the little movement they are allowed, but it's the pooling puddle under his seat that brings a smirk to my face. "What the fuck possessed you to put a bomb in my motherfucking ride?"

"The boss told me to," he blurts out.

"Which boss—my father, or my stepbrother?"

"Your father. Julio doesn't have control yet." I don't believe it, or at least there's more to the story. So there's a push from my stepbrother to take my father's spot. It's not that I didn't already see that coming, but I'm not going to let that little bitch get anywhere near the Serrano name. My family built the vineyard. That pussy's not taking that from me, no matter what he believes.

"Why would my father want me dead?" That's not something that makes sense unless his resentment has grown out of control.

"He didn't want you dead. He wanted to make you pay for your mother leaving, so he wanted your lapdog dead." He tilts his head to Fernando, who pushes himself off the wall and has his hands around his throat before Oscar can utter another word.

"Lapdog, puddle boy. I'll rip your fucking head off myself."

"Deja, Fernando. This fool is playing with the devil and doesn't even know it. No one is going to help him out of this."

"What do you mean? Your father said..." I break out in a laugh that echoes in the empty building. I hear the sound of rain on the roof as if the skies opened up so the world could clean up after me.

I lean forward and grab his face, squeezing his cheeks hard before slamming his head back and letting go. "My father's word means shit. You're dead either way. I was just deciding if I'll go slowly or fast. Frankly, at this point, it doesn't matter to me."

"He's supposed to protect me," he whines.

"Who?" I just need clarification.

"Your father."

"A dead man can't protect anyone."

"What?" he gasps.

Are you fucking kidding me? This fucker fainted. "Seriously, this pussy fainted. Get the bucket."

Fernando grabs a bucket and then walks over to the hose, filling it with ice-cold water.

"Son of a bitch," he grumbles as water splashes on his feet, which pisses him off so he launches the water into Oscar's face, shocking him awake, then in a fit of anger hits him with the bucket.

"Do you feel better?"

"A bit."

"So what does Julio have to do with all of this?"

"Nothing. He was supposed to be next."

"What?"

"After your mother, I was supposed to attack him so it would look like it was the Italians attacking his family, even the illegitimate ones."

"You tried to kill my mother."

"She didn't die either?" Oh, I've fucking had it. I whip out my gun and put slugs into his heart and head.

The two came inside, soaking wet. "Clean this up. No one comes after my family. Ever. They will pay with their lives." I storm out of the warehouse, fuming with violent need.

"At least you got the one who attacked your mother."

"That is good. Now to deal with the rest of this mess. Are you coming?"

"I'll drive." Good, because I'm not in the right frame of mind for this shit.

1

Victor
Six Years Later

"What's your plan?" Hector asks, taking a seat in front of my desk and resting his foot over his knee while I walk over to my sideboard for a drink. I look at my brother who has grown into a man over the past six years. With a degree in finance, I made him my personal accountant and the treasurer for the organization. Having seen the fucked-up side to the supposed legal workings, he made his choice to come back and work alongside me.

"I'm going to see if it's worth doing business with the Americans," I say, taking a sniff of my new bottle of the latest wine from our vineyard.

"I went to school there. The mafia's in thick with the politicians and is hiding in plain sight. Depending on what you're willing to pay, you can have anything you want," he grumbles, twisting his lips to the side while I pour us a drink.

Passing a glass to him, I sit in the same spot where I ended my father's life, although this seat is my own. As the head of the Serrano family, I've made some changes: one of them was my father's tacky office. For God's sake, the old fuck had had a pinup poster of a naked woman on the back of the door like a teenage boy. My father partied harder than he worked, leaving me to clean up the mess, put the Sicilians in their place, and rebuild trust in my men.

It's been a rocky six years with a lot of bloodshed, but we made peace once the heir took over for the Vitali family. Not that I trust him, but a détente is for the best. They're out of our territory, and they know never to cross me or the price will be more than they can afford to pay.

Now, I need to ensure that no one, and I mean no one, tries to come at us when my companies are taking off so well.

"You're probably right, but I won't let the damn Sicilians see even the slightest sign of weakness."

"There's another Spanish crew in the north that are inching closer and closer to our town."

I rake my hand through my hair, then stand. "I know. I don't want a war with these rat bastards, but I will—if they don't get fucking lost, I'll make them disappear." Pacing my office, I consider my options. There aren't many, because my father made us appear so weak that I take all acts against us seriously. We come at you full force, whether it is with guns blazing or clearing all your assets electronically, and we won't stop until we're satisfied. "I'm ready for anything. War or peace, the Serrano family will come out ahead."

"You're right, brother. Are you going to see Mama before you go?" He shares a frown with me. Last week, my mother was diagnosed with heart disease. She's not taking good care of herself and won't let us hire someone to tend to her. The woman is as strong as she is stubborn.

"Yes. I need to try to convince her to take her meds."

"It's all his fault that she's sick. If I could, I'd dig him up and shoot him again. Her heart wants to call it quits after years of abuse," Hector says, shaking his head. I sit on the edge of my desk facing my little brother. At twenty-three, Hector's determined to prove himself.

"I know. I know. It doesn't help that we haven't given her grandbabies and that all of Dad's bastard children have tons of kids."

"That's because some of them are as fucked up as our dad." Some of my half brothers hate us and would love to take the spot they feel they deserved. Blood or not, if they overstep their bounds, I pop all those assholes.

"I'm glad we buried that fuck." I'd gladly do it again. I haven't regretted it and never will.

"Damn right. Now, if you'll excuse me, I have a meeting with Guadalupe." Lupe's our winery manager who lives and breathes wine. Our last manager bailed out shortly after the bombing, claiming it was too dangerous for him. I was glad to see him go. Weak men like that bail when shit gets real, and I don't have time to deal with people like him. I let him go, but he'll never work for my family again.

"Make sure everything is running smoothly. I'll tell

Mama you'll be around later." He constantly checks in on her because like me, he wants to keep her safe while giving her the independence she craves.

"Gracias." We stand, and I pull my little brother in for a hug.

"Take care. Call me for anything," I remind him. It's not like I can do a lot from the States, but I want to know my mother's okay.

"You know I will." We walk out, and my guards go with me while my brother's men follow him out. Fernando meets me in the garage with more information that we need for our trip.

"Are you ready?" I ask, tucking my keys in my pocket. The weather's not bad today, but it's fucking shit in the States.

"Yes. Your bags have been loaded, and the weather is finally clear for travel." We were supposed to leave two days ago, but first we were hit with some torrential rain, and then they were slammed with threats of hurricanes and large swells. I have a short window before the next storm comes knocking on the Eastern Seaboard of the United States. It's now or never.

"Please stop at my mother's before we go to the airport," I tell him, although he already knew I'd want to stop there before we leave.

"Of course, Victor." I drop my head back on the headrest and relax. Having this conversation with my mother isn't something I want. I hate having to leave her when she's so sick. The fear of losing her is real for my brother and me. My phone buzzes with an email from my lawyer. The acquisition of a property in Calabria was successful. I plan to build another restaurant and brewery in that spot. Bringing a smile to my face, I inform Fernando of the news. "The spot in Calabria is ours."

"Congrats, Victor. Maybe this deal with the Americans will be necessary."

"It will save us a lot of time and money without having to go through customs."

"And other suppliers. They've been known to bust up shipments 'by accident' to help their other connections."

"You make a valid point."

"Sir, we're here." I nod, glancing out the window before stepping out of the vehicle. That woman is going to be the death of me. I see her out on her swing, and she's on her feet in a flash. I adjust my suit jacket to hide my gun and then walk to greet my mother.

"Mijo," my mother says, throwing her arms out for a hug as I step up to her portico.

"What are you doing outside by yourself?" I grumble, hugging her tightly and lifting her off her feet. With a kiss on her cheek, I set her down. My mother is petite, maybe five feet tall, and just a waif of a woman now. She needs someone cooking for her.

She leans back in my arms and slaps my chest. "I have Vicente here. I'm fine. No one has come or gone up that road until you pulled up, so you must relax. You won't need any enemies to take you down when you give yourself a stroke."

I surrender and release her. "Fine. You know I don't like you staying here all alone."

"Don't start. Come inside for some coffee and some

food before you leave." She pats my chest and takes my hand, dragging me along like a little boy into the house.

I stop just outside her front door. "Mama. Tell me you didn't cook for me."

"I'll always cook for my baby." She pinches my cheek and walks inside. Standing guard is Vicente. He's one of my younger guards, but he's been with the family for eight years.

"You don't have to cook anymore. We have a cook waiting to make you anything you'd like. You should be resting and enjoying only the best life has to offer," I say, watching her work by the stove stirring some eggs into a pan.

"I know you mean well, Victor. Pero estoy contenta."

"It doesn't change how I feel about it. You are all alone."

"Well, when you bring me some babies to care for, then I won't be alone."

"If I ever give you grandbabies, you can move back into the house."

"The day you do, I'll consider it. That house has memories I wish to forget."

I nod, knowing that she has a great point. Her scars run deeper than mine. I take a seat with a cup of coffee as she prepares a plate of breakfast for me. I'm grateful that I haven't eaten yet today because I could never pass up her cooking. She flits around the kitchen cleaning up and then brings her coffee to the table and sits.

"You must be leaving soon, si?"

"Yes. I only intend on staying in New York for two days to settle business with a shipping company." I blow on my papas con huevo before taking a bite. I can never resist her cooking.

"Take your time. Take a vacation, find a wife," she presses. Breakfast always comes at a price. The same price, actually. A family. She wants me to find someone that makes me happy and start to build on it, but it's not like she's going to fall into my lap and I'm gonna trust her with my heart and my secrets.

"I doubt it works that easily," I remind her.

"It's a big city and there are lots of women there. I have hope that you'll find the one and just know." She's a bit of a romantic. I'm not sure how she can have such an outlook given her past, but I don't want to dissuade her from a bit of joy.

"The woman I marry will be my only one. I won't be my father, so it may take forever to find the one to rule at my side."

"You're a good man, but you're not even looking for a woman."

"Hardly, Mama, but I will not be him," I vow. Everything I do has been to prove I'm not him. I might run a less-than-legal empire, but it's not a purely selfish rule. I take care of my village as well as those I employ. It's more about protecting what I have than expanding.

"Good. Then you better get going. The sooner you meet a woman, the better."

"Grandbabies. Always grandbabies." I finish my plate and get up before she can set it in the sink. I see her bag of medicine on the counter.

"Tomas su medicina?" I ask, waving the still folded bag.

"No. I don't like the feeling it gives me." She stands and snatches it from my hand.

"Mama, we aren't ready to lose you."

Setting it on the counter, she claps her hands to her hips. "I'm sorry, but I want to go on my own terms, and it's not yet. I'm made of more than that. I've never had control of my own life. First my father owned me and then sold me like chattel to your father, only to be at his mercy until his death."

"I know. We just love you so much." I wrap her up in a tight embrace.

"I know I've put you in a difficult spot." She attempted to love my father, to make it a good marriage, but he wouldn't stand for it. Everything was his way and solely for his benefit.

"No, you have not. That bastard of a father did. I only get along with Maria Luisa."

"As you should. I just cannot." I don't hold any blame on her for anything.

I pull back while still holding her at arm's length. "And you don't have to get along with any of them, but promise me that you're going to do your best to stay well whilst I'm gone, por favor."

"Por supuesto."

I kiss her and leave. I steal a glance back as we pull out of the driveway.

"She's going to be fine, Victor." Fernando is usually right, but as a son, I must always be concerned about her well-being.

"I hope so." I check my watch and send a text to my pilot. **Ten minutes out.**

"I have the file on the families when you're ready to review it."

"Have you gone through it yourself?" Fernando's team created the file and I'm certain he saw most of it, but as the head of security, he's too busy to gather the intel himself.

"Yes. Intriguing and a bit worrisome."

"How so?" I've been keeping busy with the growing tensions from the pressure of a new rival inching closer.

"They're in the middle of a shake-up and our host had a huge part to play in it." He hands me the file, and I start to read the front page. It's a report with a small picture of Santino and Giada Benedetti. He's kissing her temple as they sit at a restaurant. The notes under the picture read: *Son of the former boss of the Marchetti family, Rafael Marchetti. Killed half brother Rafael Jr. in self-defense while in Santino's company office. Giada is the daughter of Antonio Avanti.*

"We'll discuss it on the plane," I grumble, closing the file. I never realized how difficult it was to read in a moving vehicle, and we've just hit a bumpy patch of road.

"Remind me to have that repaired as soon as possible." Hard rains can damage the road quickly, and we just had a heavy storm.

Fernando nods in the rearview mirror as we hit the straightaway to the private airstrip. Once we pull up to the spot, his second in command, Luis, who followed behind with two others, helps unload our luggage. "Gracias," I say. They will fear me, but I want their respect and loyalty.

We shake hands, and then Fernando and I board the plane and meet with Ernesto, my pilot. "Hola, Jefe."

"Hola, Ernesto. How long until we land in New York?" I'm already anxious to return. I'm not one for going to the States. To me, there's nothing special about it. I have everything the American dream can offer, and our history is much richer. I prefer traveling to Europe if I wish to have a vacation, which in all honesty, I do not.

"Nine hours, as long as the weather holds."

"Bueno. We're ready when you are."

He nods and says, "Okay. We'll take off in five minutes. Please take a seat and buckle up." He swiftly turns around and heads into the cockpit while my men and I take our seats.

A few minutes later, we're up in the air and the seat belt warning turns off. The flight attendant is Ernesto's daughter, Delia. "Can I bring you anything to drink, Señor Serrano?"

"Please bring us some bourbon. Don't forget to ask them as well." She's new, and I want her to do a good job. My men know not to flirt with her, so I want her to get comfortable. She's a good girl and ready to start college soon. The men are sitting away from Fernando and myself as we discuss matters that are just between the two of us. I bring out the file on the American families and place it on the table between us.

"So tell me what these pages don't," I say, clapping my hands on my thighs and rubbing them back and forth twice over.

"The tensions are high. The Marchetti family no longer exists. Santino and his security team wiped them out over a short time while stealing the wife of his brother. Despite having the makings of a great mob boss, he's not a part of that life. He ended their reign and moved on with his life. His wife is expecting, and his associate has taken the reins to start his own operation."

I don't respond because Delia's back with our drinks. "Would you care for the in-flight meal?"

"Yes, but please give us a couple of hours." The men ate before they picked me up, so we have plenty of time before the next meal. She nods and leaves us.

"This Johnny fella?" I ask, continuing our conversation.

"Yes. He's got ties to the Irish in Boston. Santino's also been working with the Russians."

"Damn. Are you sure he's not running something underground? Getting his hands into different pots?"

"Not from what we see. It's only been a few weeks since Rafael Marchetti has been arrested."

"Well, then, we're going to need more information before we contact them. I don't trust Avanti, but he's looking for allies so we'll see what he has to offer. At least there's a party tonight. Perhaps some of them will be there. If there's a shake-up they'll be looking for lifelines and we'll hear whispers." I don't want to deal with these people for anything other than shipping, but I also need to be aware of who my enemies are.

"I have your back either way," he reminds me.

I raise my glass to him. "I'm grateful to have you at my side." I toss the bourbon back and then we go back to the plan.

My men pick up our rental SUV while Fernando and I wait. I refused the offer for their men to meet us because frankly, I don't trust getting into vehicles with strangers, especially men who operate openly on the other side of the law. We put the address to Avanti's estate into the navigation system. There's a decent amount of traffic, but we make good time.

We arrive at the closed gates and are escorted into Avanti's home before his guests arrive for their party. I freshen up in my guest room while my men do the same in the room next door. I tug on my cuffs as I check over my appearance. Strong and powerful as always, which is exactly what I am despite my current situation. With my plans waylaid, I'm at the mercy of my host. Our meeting was to happen yesterday, but due to the severe weather, my flight had been delayed.

If I had arrived on time, I would have been out of here three hours ago instead of waiting for our meeting, which rankles my nerves. I'm not the type to be waiting for anyone, especially a mediocre criminal. He's one step above the politicians in this city, but without the clout. I want access to the coastlines without restrictions, and Avanti has the connections I'm interested in.

My mother's illness made matters worse. I wouldn't have taken the trip if she had not insisted on it. She might not approve of my life, but she understands it and loves how I've taken over my father's empire while feeding him to the vultures.

Still, my mother deserved more than she had been given and I've tried to make up for the past, but some damage can't be undone. Her father sold her like chattel to my father for rights to his vineyard.

My brother and I were the only children she had before miscarrying three more times. My father had six other children with his mistresses. I hate what he did to her, parading his little leftovers with his mistresses in her face. Most of my half siblings hated him as well because they were the bastard children who were only used to promote his virility. He wanted nothing to do with them, just like he hadn't with us. Now, I own everything from both sides of the law and will one day have someone to pass it all down to, although that doesn't look to be happening soon. At least, not soon enough for my mother.

If I ever marry, I'll never betray my wife. Fuck that noise. The damage had killed my mother's heart and ruined her happiness. With all my power and money, I can't get her to take the treatment. She wants to go on her own terms, and I'm not ready for that. Being here and not by her side only brings my pain and rage to the forefront of my mind. I need to get this meeting over with and head back to Spain in the morning.

I send up a silent prayer that she'll come to her senses and get the treatment she needs before it's too late. My phone buzzes, and it's a message from the woman. **Stop worrying. I'm well. Do what you have to. Maybe meet a beautiful girl.**

I shake my head and whisper, "How does she know?"

As the head of the Serrano family, I have an

obligation to the organization to keep the empire running smoothly. I decided to up my own actions to show my strength.

"Your mother?" Fernando says, coming into the room.

"You know it." I roll my eyes and then go back to adjusting my tie. "Is my pilot ready to go in the morning?" I ask.

"He's ready as soon as you are. The plane has been refueled and stocked. Ernesto is sleeping with his phone in the hangar as he waits for your call."

"Good. I don't want to be here any longer than necessary." I didn't get more than a two-minute call from Avanti when I landed. "Avanti makes my stomach turn. He's weak and troubled. Maybe I should have contacted one of the other families."

The sound of footsteps stops all conversation, and then there's a steady knock on the door. Fernando walks over and grabs the handle, opening the door just enough to look out. "Can I help you?" His tone is brisk with the guy.

"Signor Avanti has a message for Señor Serrano." Fernando closes the door and then looks at me. I give him the nod to open it to one of Avanti's men. I take him in, and he's not as large as most of Avanti's guards and most definitely not as large as Fernando or myself.

"Señor Serrano, Signor Avanti will see you in ten minutes, although he asks that you be informed of tonight's festivities."

"Festivities?" I'm not in the mood to celebrate shit. I want to do business, and that's it. I made it clear that I had no interest in attending.

"Yes. This is the annual Virgin Sale." My eyes widen, and rage slams hard into my chest. This fucker deals in that kind of business. Immediately, I'm ready to leave and say fuck the deal. I'll find a different shipper.

"Virgin Sale?" He can see the disgust in my voice, so he continues quickly with a hint of annoyance.

"Yes. The party begins as the guests arrive. You can purchase one night with a virgin via their handlers. Guests are free to negotiate the deals and depart to participate in the transaction."

"That's fucking disgusting," I bark out, causing the little guy to flinch. Good. Let him feel my wrath.

He gains his composure just enough to continue his warning. "It is a profitable business that Mr. Avanti would hate to have ruined. If you do not purchase a lady for the evening, that is fine, but no one is allowed to depart before midnight or before every female has been purchased. If you do purchase a woman, all sales are final."

Who the fuck does he think he is?

"Where is Avanti now? I need to speak with him immediately." I don't wait a second before brushing past the man, storming out of my room and down the grand staircase with my man and his following behind me. I already know where to find the bastard. He's in his office surrounded by two of his men, sitting down in his chair with his feet kicked up on his desk. Damn, what a fool. I could have unloaded on him from that position, even with his guards. They barely move when I enter the room. They should have flinched. Fernando would have been prepared and had his gun out on someone's head.

"Hello, Avanti. Can we discuss business privately?"

He drops his feet off his desk and then grabs his glass. "This is as private as it gets for now. You look a little heated, Serrano. Why don't you have a drink and settle down?"

"I'll pass on the drink and the pussy. I thought this was a party and not a prostitution ring," I bark out while Avanti straightens his tie. Two of his men stand guard, eyeing me as if I'm a threat. I am, but I'm not stupid enough to do it without a plan. I might not like Avanti, but I have no reason to end his life—yet. Anyone that messes with my business isn't left to talk about it, and should anything go wrong tonight, I will kill him easily.

He leans back in his chair, smug as possible while holding a glass of cheap scotch without a care in the world, rankling me even more. "Relax, Serrano. These women are here on their own accord. They want money, and we want pussy. Don't you?"

Unlike this sick bastard, I have standards, and that doesn't include paying for sex. The man has a wife, but I bet he'd screw as many of these women as he could. He's just like my father, and that turns my disgust to hatred quickly. "I have no interest in participating in this. I don't pay for pussy. I came to talk about my exports and nothing more."

My temper's hot. I'm on the cusp of telling him the fuck off, but it's not wise at this juncture. "We have time to discuss this in the morning. You can stay in your room for the night if you don't want to spend some pocket change, but I assure you some of these little morsels are worth the money."

Fury rips through me. My time is money, and here I am wasting time. This fucker believes that he can get me to stay like I'm not the head of my own family. I'll cancel the deal and shoot this prick in the face when he's least expecting it. I don't care if I lose the money. Never once have I had moral qualms when it comes to the people I deal with, but something about this whole selling of a barely legal girl's virginity makes my stomach churn.

"I'll be in my room." I walk out of the office without another look at that poor excuse for a man, and then catch something out of the corner of my eye. The party has already started with well-dressed people all around. I can't hide my disgust until I see her.

I'm able to take her in from head to toe before she sees me: a petite blonde whose eyes pull me in. My first thought is that she's mine, but that's nuts. I watch how the short black dress barely covers her ass and her large tits nearly spill out of the top. The urge to cover her up strikes me. I push away that feeling because I didn't come here for any woman.

Something in her look screams that she's not ready for this party. Does she have second thoughts? She just entered through the main entrance with a man at least twice her age. The diamond around her neck reflects in the room, perfect for gaining any man's attention. She's going to be snapped up quickly like that. That idea doesn't sit well with me. It doesn't sit well at all. Fucking hell. She's going to ruin my morals. I have to get away before it's too late.

2

Dove

I RUN the straightener through my hair unsteadily, leaving parts with a wave and a crease so I'll have to redo that section again, further aggravating my father because it's taking too long for him. It's not intentional, but his presence just outside the bathroom door unnerves me, causing my already tense body to shake. This whole situation makes my stomach roll. It's bad enough that I haven't eaten since I had a small bowl of oatmeal this morning, but I'm not allowed to eat until this is all over because he doesn't want to risk me looking bloated. I'm just one hundred and twenty pounds, most of the weight in my boobs and butt.

"I can't do this," I complain, knowing that it's pointless because he's not going to change his mind and I have no way of escaping. I don't just mean our tiny hole-in-the-wall apartment, but out of town. He's made sure I have no other recourse but to go along with this illegal, immoral, super-expensive prostitution.

"You don't have a choice. You have to do this, or they'll kill us both," my father shouts through the pressed wood door that separates the bathroom from his bedroom. I've got a hit on my head if I don't make a lot of money tonight. That knowledge sends a chill up my spine and is the only thing driving me to look my best.

Yesterday he showed me the text message with the threat in it as a reminder that my life hangs in the balance.

Dove follows through or both of you will be chopped up after we take her for free.

I told him we should go to the police, but he told me they own the police, which isn't hard to fathom. Money and power shape this world, and I have neither of those. Now I'm getting ready to sell my innocence to the highest bidder in order to pay off his debt. Not even my debt—his debt. My father, Donatello Falcone, is the epitome of greed and excess, wanting things he can't have and buying stuff with money he doesn't earn. The more he gets, the less he feels satisfied. He can sell me now, but once I'm used up, his bargaining chip will be gone.

"Do you need to see it again?" The threat is laced in his voice. If I fail to go through with this, we both die. He's worried about his own skin, not mine. I've been expendable since the day my mother died. He would have gotten rid of me then, but she left a small trust to be used for my care. Every penny has been spent, and not on me.

"No." A shiver runs through me as I consider the

alternative. If I go to this party, I'll be sold like a piece of meat for one night, or door number two, I get raped and murdered if I don't. I suppose staying alive is my only option, so it's the reality I have to accept.

I continue to work on my hair and listen to him pace outside the door—as if that's going to help me get ready any faster. Now that my hair is finally completely straight, I unplug the flat iron I got for twenty bucks at the CVS. He gave me just a hundred dollars to get dolled up, as he put it. I can't leave it down because they want my slender neck and shoulders on display, so I give myself the Ariana Grande hairstyle, straight and tight with a slight twist.

"I doubt anyone is going to buy me for half a million dollars." He's truly got to be out of his mind to think that my virginity is worth that much. I'm so damned inexperienced, it would probably be a terrible event. He'd want a damn refund, but I can't get back my innocence. Hell, who am I kidding? The only thing that remains of my vestiges of childhood innocence is my virginity. I've spent years learning the ins and outs of shady dealings.

"You never know. Besides, they said I only need to come up with two-fifty. I'm sure your virginity is worth that at least. Some of these fuckers are twisted and get a kick out of it." *Says the man whoring out his daughter.* If I weren't afraid of being killed, I would have told him to shove the idea up his ass, but a girl's gotta do what a girl's gotta do to stay alive.

"Fine. Is this okay?" I ask, stepping out of the bathroom to show him the outfit. We live in a one-bedroom apartment that costs more than it's worth, and my bedroom is the sofa. We have very little to no privacy.

"Well, if you weren't my daughter, I'd pay that much for you." I try not to throw up from that comment and go back into the bathroom and close the door, making sure to flip the lock. He's never given me that pedo-incest vibe, but I wouldn't put anything past him once I'm not worth as much. God, I have to make my escape. I'm not afraid that he'll come after me, but I am scared shitless that Caesar Avanti will hunt me down even after he kills my father. It's the only reason I don't make a run for it.

I look myself over in the mirror and I do look good, but now I get an icky vibe about it. I straightened my long blonde hair and put it up in a tight ponytail on the back of my head, wrapping a braided strand around the tie to add elegance to a quick style. My sexy, vibrant red lipstick is the eight-hour kind that stays on until rubbed off. The only other makeup I add is a voluminous mascara to accentuate my eyes. Hopefully it does the trick. My pimp out there didn't want me to look overdone because some of these old creeps got a kick out of innocent girl-next-door types.

"Before we leave, put this on." He hands me a fancy long black jewelry box. I open it up and see a gorgeous teardrop diamond necklace. It's stunning, shimmering in the light with pure radiance.

"Why can't you pawn this?" I say, shoving it at him with a little more force than I expected out of myself as disgust fills me.

He grabs my arm roughly, but not hard enough to leave a permanent mark, and then snarls in my face. "Little shit, this is a gift from the host to attract buyers to your rack. Behave and put it on like a good girl," he hisses, grabbing my hand and slapping the box in it with enough force to sting. I don't let him know it hurt.

Asshole. I don't say anything or show any signs that I'm afraid; instead, I slip on the necklace like it's nothing but a trinket. The diamond teardrop dips like an arrow pointing directly to my cleavage, which is ample in this dress even without a bra. Fuck. I'm going to be sold tonight, even if it's not for the money he wants. I look expensive.

"Good. Now you look like a pricey commodity." He winks and clicks his tongue, emphasizing my valuable status. I hate him more than I ever have before, which I didn't believe possible. I send up a silent prayer that someone will save me from this nightmare, but I know that's never going to happen. My life has been one terrible year after another to the point of being sold like a piece of property.

"Let's go. We don't have time to waste. I want to make sure you are picked up before they run out of money." I reach for my coat, but he shakes his head. "Not that trash over that dress. I want you on display, looking expensive."

He hands me my shawl, which isn't warm enough for the changing weather and the cold front that showed up after the last hurricane warning.

We're taking his brand-new car that cost one hundred thousand dollars. Who the hell needs an expensive car in the middle of freaking New York City when you live in a shoebox condo that's seen better days? He can't hock his precious things, just his daughter's innocence.

I barely have a light wrap over my shoulders even though it's the middle of September and the weather's getting chilly. My teeth chatter as we step out onto the NYC sidewalk outside our condo building. We don't have a valet or our own parking garage next to the building, so we have to walk to the car. In my high heels and short dress, I look like he just bought me for the night. I get a couple of whistles and a honk before we make it to the car. He's not even the slightest bit of a gentleman enough to get the door for me, so I gently swing it open, making sure not to hit the curb or I'll pay big time after the night's over, and I climb into the passenger seat. "Shit," I screech; the leather's practically frozen to my skin. Seeing my instant distress, he flips the heat on because we can't have me catching a cold before we get there.

"Calm down. You're acting like a baby." The way he brushes off my chattering teeth as nothing sends me into a rage I've never felt before.

"Says the man fully fucking clothed. How about you put on a dress and see if your balls don't shrivel up," I snap out, letting his attitude, the situation, and the cold change my tone. Not only do I have to suffer the indignity of being used, but I have to freeze all the way there.

"Watch your mouth."

I laugh. This is the only time I'll get away with saying anything to him. "Why? What are you going to do? It's not like you're going to lose out on a huge payday by bruising me up."

"Just wait until this is all over, and you'll regret the day you were born," he says through clenched teeth, itching to beat me.

I roll my eyes. "Been there, done that. Just remember it's not you I'm afraid of. You've hurt me more than anyone else could, but I let those petty sentiments go long ago. It's the Avanti organization that has me going through this violation because I want to live."

"You will fear me. Trust me on that." I sense there's more to his threat, but I don't give a shit at the moment.

I roll my eyes again, cross my arms, and twist my torso to look out the window, refusing to acknowledge anything he has to say. With my sudden silence, he pulls out into wall-to-wall traffic. Again, pointless to own a car in this mess.

We're headed out to Long Island to an estate in the Hamptons. The drive seems to be the absolute quickest in history. I suppose that the whole theory of relativity holds some merit as I brace myself for what's about to unfold.

We pull into a massive, gated estate that has limos and SUVs lined up one after another, waiting for their turn. When we finally arrive at the front of the line, I'm shaking from the sheer fear of what's to come. A valet assists me out of the car, and another takes the keys from my father. Another gentleman who arrives at the same time as we do takes an appraising look at me and then says something in another language that I can't make out, and then we're escorted up the steps where my father shows our special invitation to be let in. Apparently, they invite people from around the world to this event. I hope the foolish bastard that buys my innocence at least speaks English and isn't completely ancient, or worse, absolutely gross looking.

As soon as we walk in, my hopes are dashed. Everyone is older than my father; most are old enough to be my grandfather. It doesn't take long for me to see the truth of my situation, and it takes everything in me to keep the bile down. There are a couple of guys that are better looking than others, but mostly it's a bunch of ugly, overweight men who probably have wives and kids. I can't imagine them over me sweating and grunting, touching my body. They're going to need a bunch of lube to get me wet enough and a lot of alcohol, which I plan to have.

I shudder in revulsion and fear. *What am I doing here?*

I need to get away from my father and out of this place. I search the room for the exits as my fight-or-flight has kicked in. The chances of me getting away depend on if I can get away from my father. Sensing my change of heart or just not trusting me, he intensifies the already firm grip on my arm that I doubt he's going to loosen until I'm sold.

I'm trying to keep my head down so that I don't attract any attention, but my father isn't having any of that either. He grabs my chin hard, forcefully turning my head to him and whispers, "Keep your head up. No one can see your fucking face. Remember, it's your head that's on a platter as well as mine. Now, smile like a good hooker."

That's the only reason I'm here, I remind myself. I don't give a crap if they put a bullet in his head or whatever it is these people do. It's my life I want to preserve. After this is over, I plan to run and start a life of my own somewhere else far from these evil fuckers. Then his next bailout will have to come from someone else, or he'll be food for worms.

Fighting back the tears, I decide right there that I'm

going to carry myself with dignity. After all, it's just sex, and I'm betting probably very short sex. I straighten my back, stiffen my shoulders, and hold my head up high. I'm going to meet my fate like a warrior.

With lips plump and determination on my face, I scan the room, hoping for a good-looking pervert. That's when I spot the *one* man in this place who I wouldn't mind being whored out to. I'm practically salivating because he's so good looking. I shouldn't care because he's just as foul as the rest of these men, but goodness, my heart's pounding all the way down to my pussy as if my body's vibrating.

He's tall, maybe six four. His broad shoulders scream muscular like he doesn't wear a suit most days. He's clearly well built in an all-black suit and tie, and he wears it well. He's older than me, but not as old as the rest or even my father. From this distance, it's hard to see if there is gray hair in his thick, slicked-back dark hair.

My eyes just seem to have a mind of their own as I stare at him from head to toe. My behavior is no better than any man in this place, but still, I can't stop staring at his stern jawline with a hint of stubble coming in that makes me wonder what it would feel like to run my hand over it. I rake my eyes over him, admiring his well-built torso like a woman with experience and hunger. I can't seem to pull my eyes away.

As I move my attention lower, a specific part of his frame catches my interest. A profound desire pools between my legs. I'm not even sure when I became such a pervert, but I'm staring straight at his cock. Maybe it's because it's hard to miss even with the dark suit. My tongue slips out of my mouth, and it's only after his eyes narrow on me that I realize that I'm eye fucking him. I've only heard about and seen eye fucking in movies or read about it in books. It's intensely wrong and right at the same time, and my body craves more.

Several of the girls are already making their way to him, vying for the prime rib mixed with a bunch of freezer-burned chicken. They're all thinking the same thing I am. If we're selling ourselves, we might as well be with a man who doesn't make us sick to look at. Hell, I might use him as my fantasy because there's no way he'd pick me with all those beautiful women clamoring to get closer to him.

A waiter passes by and smiles at me. I smile politely back and refuse the drink he's offering. "A drink, my pet?" he asks, attempting to flirt with me. I shake my head a second time. Earlier I thought I wanted something to calm my nerves, but now I want my head clear so I can record the memory of the stranger perfectly in my mind.

My father ignores my refusal, snatches a wine glass off the tray, and hands me the drink. "Drink. It'll calm your ass down." I take it and close my eyes and hold my nose, drinking it down in one long swig. It tastes funky, but at least it's over with.

Strangely, I want another drink. I'm going to need all the liquid courage I can get to make it through the night. When I turn my attention to the sexy beast, he's scowling at me, proving that I've gotten my hopes up for nothing. He's pissed that I've even turned my gaze onto him again. Fuck it.

I turn around and I'm immediately greeted by a guy a

lot less attractive, and of course his eyes are running up and down my body. He has to be in his late fifties or early sixties, balding and pudgy around the middle. "How much are you going for?"

A waiter passes by and I steal another glass, drinking it before he can walk away. I set it on the tray, reaching for another when my father pushes my hand down forcefully. "Be on your way," he informs the server.

I don't know what to say to the man waiting for an answer because I'm not interested, but my father answers for me. "Five hundred K."

My stomach lurches at the idea of him being the one to steal my virginity. He reaches out, cuffing my bicep. "I'll take—"

"Your fucking hands off of her right now if you want to take another damn breath." I look up to see the scowling sexy bastard from earlier. He's glaring at the spot where the guy's hand is on my arm. He tugs me out of the guy's grip before the man has a chance to let go.

He grabs my hand and leads me away from both men. My hand tingles in a flush of electricity so profound that I hold tight and I don't want to let go. Another man with a hint of grey at his temples arches his brow, giving him a strange look, but all my captor does is nod and the man's expression changes. They share a brief conversation, but I don't hear anything except the pounding of my own heart. The wine must be going to my head or maybe it's his touch—either way, I feel euphoric.

He doesn't say a word as we walk quickly upstairs and then down a corridor.

"Excuse me, but where are you taking me?" I ask

foolishly. Obviously, he wants to get what he's paying for. Suddenly I hate him, and yet I want him at the same time. How is that even possible? He's my best option, and yet I know that I'm nothing but a conquest on his belt. He must have some serious issues to pay that much money for a virgin. It's not like I'm going to be any good.

"To bed," he bites out through clenched teeth without slowing his movements.

"But..." I stammer, unsure of what to say. I'm not sure what I expected, but something about him gives me hope that this won't be a bad experience. So far, he's stiff and seems angry at me like I'm the one forcing him, while I'm being dragged along.

He stops in front of a door where another man in a suit stands. Shit—he's not going to invite that man to have me too? "Make sure no one tries to get in here. I want privacy." He opens it and leads me inside.

"But..."

"But what? You want that money given to your handler, right?" he asks, slamming the door closed and leaning on it as if I'm going to escape.

"I do, but..."

He locks the door and then walks over to the bar, pouring a glass of a dark liquid and then taking it over to a large chair in the corner of the room. "Speaking of butts—strip." A low grunt escapes his throat as he rakes his eyes over my body. His stern voice demands I comply while my own need screams for me to submit. Who is this woman, and what happened to the prude I used to be?

"I've never done this before," I tell him as I grab the strap of my dress.

He scoffs. "I sure as fucking hope not or there's going to be a lot of dead bodies around." Of course he'd be pissed since he spent a fortune on my virginity. "What's your name?"

"Dove Falcone. And you?" I'm sure he's not going to tell me so as not to create a familiarity between us, and yet I need to know, although I can't explain why it's important.

"Victor Serrano. From this moment on, you're going to do everything I say." A shiver runs through me in the most delightful way, even though I know it's wrong—so wrong.

3

Victor

I TAKE the steps up the wide staircase at a light jog when the insane urge returns and becomes unbearable. Something in me begs me to investigate the electricity that jolts toward me when I see her, but still I ignore it. There's nothing here for me, and most certainly not something I'd pay to have. *I didn't come here to buy a young lady's virginity,* I remind myself. I think it's fucking disgusting, but I came to make a deal with one of the Italian mobsters in America. A criminal who's willing to sell her to the most eager old dick.

Shaking my head, the thought of someone else touching her only adds to my fury at this entire situation.

I scan the crowd, looking for her as a group of young ladies stare in my direction, inching closer. I can tell what they're thinking; unfortunately, they're going to be sorely disappointed. I'm the youngest man in the room and considered the most handsome by far, but I'm not interested.

Finally, my eyes land on my little beauty in a cheap black dress again; I'm floored by the desire she stirs in me. Suddenly, an idea strikes that I can use to justify my actions—she'll be the one to give me heirs.

I watch and grow more and more furious at the scene before me. The way her fucking pimp has his hand on her chin and then forces her to drink pisses me off. I'm already halfway there when a stupid fucker dares to put his hands on her. He touches what belongs to me. I could kill him, and that makes me angrier. Where has this possessive rage come from? Why her? She's beautiful and sexy, but she's probably ten years younger than me. She'd be better off with Hector. I growl at that idea, immediately dismissing it as I irrationally get pissed at my brother.

Enraged, I rip her from their grasps and signaled to Fernando, who's standing guard at the edge of the steps, to come. "Pay them what you must." He looks at me with curiosity but quickly stifles any questions he has.

"Yes, sir." He nods and leaves to make the deal. One of Avanti's men approaches. "Sir, you must know there are other bidders for her. If you do not seal the deal tonight, so to speak, she may be bought out from under you."

I grab him by the collar and snarl. "She's mine." He nods and backs off. I'm not in my home country, or I'd just put a bullet in his head and move along.

I rush her back to my suite. I had no intentions of fucking anyone, but now that she's got me fucking for money, and learning that if I don't take what I paid for that someone will snatch her away, changes my intentions. I'm going to make sure I get my fill of her before I leave.

She looks so nervous, but that's not my problem. She shouldn't have looked at me with those "fuck me" eyes, and she sure as fuck did. I didn't miss the way she unconsciously licked her lips when she first spotted me. The thought of someone else buying her sets my teeth on edge so intensely that it forced my hand.

She wants to talk, but I can't stop the need to mark my motherfucking territory. The second that bastard offered for her, I was filled with blood-red fury. She's mine, and I'm going to make sure of it. "I said strip." I'm forceful with her because she's willing to sell her pussy for money. If we'd met anywhere else, I might have taken this slower, but those sons of bitches downstairs aren't going to swoop in and take her from me.

She grips the zipper on her side and pulls, biting on her bottom lip as she struggles with the damn thing. Either she was a professional liar, or she has truly never done something like this. It better be the latter or I'll destroy all those who came before me. She may be a virgin, but she could have done everything else. I have to tamp down that insanely jealous attitude. Walking up to her, I grab the front of it and tear it straight down the center. She gasps, and her perfectly perky tits bounce free. Her light pink nipples on display tighten and harden with the feel of my stare. My sweet little virgin is turned on, which is really fucking good.

She's so damn sexy that my cock jerks in my slacks, but despite the delicious sight before me, the fact that she doesn't have a bra on hasn't gone unnoticed. "If you ever walk out without a bra on again, you won't be able to sit for a month. Do you hear me?" A fierce sense of possessiveness colors my voice. Her eyes flash with desire but then calm instantly, as if she's fighting the attraction.

"Um...I'm not yours for more than the night."

I try hard not to laugh. I didn't know the exact rules for this exchange ring, but I know that one night with her will never be enough. I don't care what anyone says. "Who the fuck told you that bullshit?" I growl. Even the notion that she could leave sends a wave of emotions through me that I can't process.

"My father," she whispers, blushing a pretty pink that goes down to her throat.

As sexy as she is, my need gets a cold chill when she mentions who her fucking handler is. I break out in a chuckle because I've never been so damn disgusted than I am right now. Her sick father sold her off to the highest bidder. Me. I'm the sick fuck who bought her.

"Well, I own you. Do you think I'd pay that much for virgin pussy? Pussy's pussy." I know that's not true because looking at her, I see more than just a way to get my rocks off; I have plans for her that include so much more than a one-night stand.

"Then why buy my virginity? I'm sure it's going to be terrible." I chuckle because she sounds like she's trying to talk me out of it, but that's the furthest thing from my mind. Terrible? Not likely. I'm already throbbing and ready to blow my load.

"I need an heir, and a little innocent thing like you would be perfect. You are a virgin, aren't you?" I question.

I'm almost positive that she is, but I must hear it from her lips.

"Of course," she exclaims, crossing her arms in a huff under her breasts, pushing those magnificent tits up. My mouth waters as I picture sucking on them until she's marked up and coming apart for me, but I have questions that I need answered. I'm not sure why they matter, but they do.

"I know your pussy has never been touched, but what about these?" My finger twirls around her nipple, stiffening the tiny pale pink nub instantly. She only replies with a shake of her head that just won't do. I pinch her other nipple, sending her gaze to meet mine. "When I ask you a question, I want you to answer it out loud. Has anyone played with your tits?"

"No." I give them each a light caress for good measure. Later, I'll feast on them, but for now, I commence my interrogation.

Grabbing her wrist, I turn her palm up and bring it to my cock. "Have you touched another man's cock?" I don't even know how I got the words past my lips but I did, quickly removing her hand from my meat before I embarrass myself.

"No."

Lifting my hand to her lips, I brush my thumb over the bottom one. It's soft and plump, making me want to taste her. "What about these lips? Have you kissed another man?"

"No." Wow, I've got a lot to teach my little Dove. She created a monster and doesn't even know it.

"Good. Now, I'm going to give you your first lesson." I

cup her cheek, drop my head and taste her lips. It's light at first, and then I slip one hand through her hair, gripping the back of her neck while my other hand skims down her backside, squeezing her firm ass. Fuck, the feel, the taste of her lips goes straight to my balls. I'm harder than I've ever been, and it's just a fucking kiss. I pull back, absorbing the reaction she creates in me. I'm not sure I fucking like it. I'm vulnerable and I can't be, especially because of paid-for pussy.

I need to regain my power and control back. "On your knees. You're going to suck my cock," I command, taking a step back to create some distance.

"What? But..."

Damn it. I don't let anyone get away with talking back except my little brother, and I'm not ready to give her that fucking power over me. She's just a sexy piece of ass to use. Just saying that shit makes me feel fucked up inside. Still, I've got a job to do, and that's to get her well-bred with my heir while screaming my name. I have a feeling that a lifetime in her pussy will never be enough.

"Do you want to leave now and give yourself to that old fuck out there?" Just thinking about that bastard has calmed my dick down, but then the image of her on her back for the fucker engulfs me with hatred for him. I ought to go find him and put a bullet in his head. I make a mental note to tell Fernando to find out who he is. I'm going to destroy him one way or another.

"No." That's a good answer because I'd have to kill him anyway.

Even if she had said yes, I wouldn't have let her walk out of here to another man no matter what happened.

"Then don't make me tell you again. Knees." She looks up at me, tits rock hard, eyes curious, lips fucking plump as she lowers herself to her knees. I free him from the tight confines of my slacks; the fucker's aching to be inside her tight confines, but first, I want to punish her for turning me into this sick bastard. Paying for sex.

She stares at my thick rod that's glistening with a fuckload of cum on the tip, ready for her mouth and her tits. "Don't be afraid. Wrap those fuckable lips around it." She cranes her neck and sticks her tiny pink tongue out. The rush is insane. I'm higher than a kite with lust for Dove. Damn, she's going to be the death of me, but in my profession, it may be the best way to go. Fuck! It pisses me off how much I'm thinking with my dick, just like my father.

I push my jacket off and start to unbutton my shirt, tucking the bottom away from my dick to keep them out of her face because I'm about to get a little rough with her.

Grabbing her cheeks, I squeeze and she opens up for me. I press my thumb down inside her mouth, holding it open. Sliding my cock inside, I watch her reaction. She's not sure of herself. Her teeth scrape me a little hard, but I let it go. Soon she'll be taking my cock down like a pro. She relaxes just a bit and then fidgets. I look, and she's clenching her thighs together. "That's a good girl, suck my cock like it's the only one you get." She does as commanded, picking up the pace, gagging a little and pulling off and back on. Fuck, she's getting too good too fast. I'm going to nut down her throat in another minute.

"That's it, baby." I pull out of her sexy mouth and grab

her chin, turning it up to face me. "Did you like that?" From her squirming, I'm sure she fucking did.

She nods. I lift my brow. "Yes," she answers properly. I undo the rest of the buttons on my shirt, peeling it off and letting it fall on the floor.

"Is your pussy wet from sucking on my cock, knowing how close your sexy mouth was getting me to come down your throat? Would you like that?"

"Yes." Her eyes give away how aroused she is as I lose the rest of my clothes. Standing in front of her, naked and harder than steel, I watch her hungry appraisal.

"Part your thighs and let me see what's mine." She does what she's told and leans back on the floor, spreading her legs wide. Her wetness coats her thighs and the thin material of the black thong she's wearing. "Push your panties over and let me see that soaking wet cunt." Her fingers shake as she pushes the black lacy material to the side. Seeing her slit makes me ravenous. Bending down, I scoop her up in my arms and carry her to the bed. I grab her panties and drag them down her slender legs. Slamming her thighs open, I dip my head between her heat, breathing her untouched core. My tongue lashes at her slit. Her body flexes and a sexy gasp escapes her chest. I need more of her cries and taste.

I slip one finger into her tight channel, feeling how insanely difficult it's going to be to work my big cock inside her. I growl against her mound, knowing I'm fucking addicted to her pussy. This isn't good. I'm a man obsessed. She cries out, grabbing the sheets as she comes. I eat her release up while I pump two digits into her depths, stretching her out.

"Mine," I grunt against her snatch. Fuck, I'm in a world of trouble. "Do you like your pussy devoured like that? You need more?"

She shakes her head vigorously, forgetting the rules. I pop her pussy with my hand and then suck hard. "Yes, yes. Please make me come, Victor." She creams, coming on my face with her pussy pushing up in my face. Growling, I'm so damn hard that cum drips onto the sheets. She opens her eyes, surprised by her own response. I pump two fingers into her, doing my best to make her as wet as possible.

I pull them out of her soaking, throbbing cunt and lick her flavor off.

"Time to seal the deal." Leaning over her, I thrust my cock forward in one motion, tearing the thin membrane, making her officially mine. The feeling of pride is short-lived when I see the tears in her eyes. A part of me returns to being human for just a moment.

"The pain will pass, baby." My mouth closes on hers, kissing her until she relaxes. It feels too fucking good to continue, so I break our kiss before I nut. "Better?" I ask, reaching between us to cup her tit, squeezing her nipple.

"Yes," she answers. I pull out and then push slowly back in, hitting her cervix. The thought of splashing that fucker with my jizz and creating our family causes me to drill her pussy faster and faster. Her big tits bounce, dragging my focus to them. I can't take my eyes off of them, so I bend and suck one into my mouth, grunting and moaning while she roles her hips up, taking me deeper into her, stretching the fuck out of her little hole.

"You're so fucking sexy, little Dove," I whisper, licking her supple flesh.

"Victor," she moans.

"I'm going to fill your little pussy with my seed." I bite down, causing her to cry out and clench around my shaft. "Fuck. Take it all, Dove."

"Fill me up, Victor." She clings to me and arches her chest in my face.

I come hard into her depths.

I collapse onto her, using my elbows on the mattress to hold off my weight. Staring down at her, she blushes, and I have to take those plump, swollen lips. "Was that okay?"

"It was..." *Incredible, indescribable.* My phone rings, giving me an out before I confess my sudden addiction, so I pull out of her and go to grab it, walking into the bathroom so she doesn't hear the conversation.

It's Avanti. "What's up?"

"I need to have a word with you. It's important. I only need a minute of your time."

"Fine. It better be quick." He wants to meet downstairs, which means I need to leave her briefly. I'm flooded with indecision. I slip on my clothes and say, "Don't leave this room. I'll be back soon."

"What—are you trying to score a double-virgin night?" I refuse to dignify that with an answer because I feel guilty as fuck for what just happened.

"Behave. Shower and get back in bed." I leave the room, regretting it immediately. Leaving her alone bothers me, but what can I do? It's not like I can take her with me, especially since I shredded her clothes. After my meeting, I'll make it up to my future wife. I text one of my men and tell him to be at my door. He meets me on the stairwell. "Don't leave this door until I return. Under no circumstances is she allowed to leave. If anyone comes up here, send them on their way. Am I clear?"

"Yes, sir."

"Good. And don't fucking touch her." The thought of someone putting their hands on her makes me livid.

When I arrive at Avanti's office, he has a shit-eating grin on his face. "So you found some little morsel palatable after all?" I should have expected it, considering my vehemence and their lack of respect.

"Did you have something to impart, or are you wasting my time?"

"I saw that you bought the lovely Dove Falcone. I thought her father was nuts to put her up for so much, but it seemed you swooped in and stole her from another buyer." He can't stop smiling, and it makes me want to put a bullet in his head.

"Again. Do you have something important to say?" I ask with a hiss. With every second he wastes of mine, I get closer to pulling out my gun.

"No. The money has been received, and I'm certain from your rumpled clothes that you've made good work of that body of hers."

"Enough. Do not talk about her like a whore, or it'll be the last thing you do."

"Whoa." He holds his hands up as if he's really intimidated by me. "Relax. You know the money's only for the night."

"Yeah, well, that's good because I wouldn't give these

fuckers another dollar of my money. I'm going to take what I want. She's old enough to leave, and that's what we're doing."

"What about our business?"

"I'll be in touch." He stands up and we shake on it. I have to get to her before they try to take her from me. Leaving his office, I maintain my control but I take out my phone and message my driver to be prepared. The party's still going on, but the groupings are smaller. I avoid all of them and dash up to the guest room.

"She has not left," Marcelino says.

"Good." I open the door to find her in one of my dress shirts that goes just to the bottom of her ass, lying down on the bed, curled into a ball.

"Little Dove," I call out and wait for a response, but I don't get one. Seeing that she's asleep, I prepare to leave. I call the woman who does the gifts for my mother. She answers, even though it's only early morning there. "I need a full wardrobe and all the feminine necessities delivered to my estate before evening."

"Que tamaño, Señor Serrano?"

I pick up the torn dress and panties. "A size six with ample breast room, and the panties are a five in American sizes."

"Very well. I will get started."

"Good."

I hang up and check on Dove, who's still fast asleep and looking sexy as fuck. I don't want her to put up a fight as I take her back on my private jet, so the longer she stays asleep, the better.

"Are we ready?" Fernando and the men are getting

everything done so I can get out of here as fast as humanly possible.

"Yes, everything is ready." I scoop her up in my arms and carry her down to the SUV, carrying her away from the entrance to the party hall. I don't want to run into her father, or I might have to kill him. A light sigh comes from her parted lips, drawing my attention to them. I ache to drop my head down and take her mouth, but I can't kiss her or I'll want to shove my dick into her tiny cunt again and she's not ready for that. We wait inside with the heat on as they load up my suitcase and theirs. The money I spent on her was disgusting, but from now on, every dollar will be spent on her behalf.

Five minutes later, we're rolling out of the estate for good.

She curls into me as she sleeps, and this strange feeling hits me. I want her to be comfortable in my arms always. The anger I felt earlier shifts to its rightful place —straight at me. I'm a bastard for taking what I wanted. I used her like a whore when I knew damn well she's not. Whatever her reason for the money, I'm still the asshole who took her virginity.

I make some calls and get things done over the phone. The papers will be waiting for me the moment we step out of the car. I have to make this right for everyone, but the first step is to legally make her mine.

There are four men waiting when we arrive on the tarmac: my pilot, the judge, his assistant, and a notary.

"Thank you for being here. I want to be up and out as soon as we take our seats," I inform Ernesto, who nods and departs. Next is the judge and his notary with him to get this marriage over with.

"Sir, you know she's not in the right frame of mind to sign that," the notary says to the judge, making me want to shove my foot up his ass.

I don't wait for the judge to respond to the fuckhead. I didn't ask them to have a fucking conscience. I told them to bring me the most unscrupulous motherfuckers they had. "Do I look like I give a fuck? You're here to do one job, and that's to legalize this. I'm paying you a lot of money for it."

"Yes, Mr. Serrano." His little bitch whimper lets me know that his outburst is good and dead.

I brush her soft cheek, and she sighs sweetly. "Mi amor, I need you to wake up for a minute."

Her eyes open slightly. "Victor," she calls out and brushes her lips against my chin. Fuck, I'm standing there with her in my arms and my dick stiffer than hell trying to get her to marry me, and she has to go and do something so fucking adorable. I look up at the asshole who questioned me and give him a smirk.

"Dove, sign here." She looks up at me sleepily, smiles, and signs it, falling asleep again. I do my best to control my urge to kiss her. I sign, and the judge does his part followed by the notary. Fernando scans the document with his phone and then shows it to me. "Great. Thank you, gentlemen. My wife needs her rest." Everything happens in an instant, and we're through with the legalities without any trouble.

I shake their hands while Fernando handles the payment, and then I turn and carry my little wife onto the plane. I sit Dove down in a seat and buckle her in because we're about to take off. After giving orders to the staff to leave us be, I buckle myself in as well. The men move to the back of the plane to give us some privacy.

I do my best to focus on other things while we're in the air, but my head constantly lifts and turns to stare at the beauty beside me. God, what have I gotten myself into? I can't and won't let her go, but how the hell is this supposed to work? I reach over and brush a strand of hair away from her angelic face. She moves and sighs, but instead of waking, she snuggles deeper down into her seat. I get up and place a blanket on my little wife. I look at her and know I'm no better than my father. I exchanged money for her virginity. Still, I won't change the path we're on. We'll just have to make this work.

Seven hours into the flight, I've managed to get everything organized. I steal another glance at her for the hundredth time, and she's still sleeping. My head spins with the notion that she isn't just sleeping, but she's been doped up. I ask for a bottle of water and some medicine from the flight attendant.

I gently wake her up and give her the meds and water. It takes her a moment to shake off the fog, and then she's frantic.

4

Dove

I FEEL warm and comfortable as I wake up. My eyes slowly open—and then fly open when I see I'm not in my bed but instead in a chair on a plane. Panic sets in, and I look around to see Victor. I try to remember everything from the night before. Damn, did I lose my virginity to a player last night? I look up, and he's on his laptop. Did he drug me? I search my arms for needle marks and pain, but there's nothing there.

"Ah, little Dove. You are awake. How are you feeling?" He reaches up to touch me, and I flinch as I try to figure out what's happening.

"What's going on? Where are we going? Why am I on a plane?" I screech, my eyes darting around the room and then back to him when he cups my chin, halting my movements instantly.

His green eyes gently stare into mine like he's trying to tame a wild animal. Like magic, I'm starting to settle down. "Calmate, mi esposa. We should be landing in Madrid in an hour."

My mind runs in circles as I process that information. "Madrid as in Madrid, Spain?"

"Yes. I told you that you would be the mother of my children," he says, as if it's no big deal. I thought it was sex talk. People get off on dirty, wild shit.

"What?" The room begins to sway, and everything goes dark.

"Amor, por favor. Abra sus ojos. Mi esposa. Dove, wake up." This time, I'm in Victor's arms as I come to. Our eyes meet, and he releases a sigh of relief before his body tenses up.

"I'm going to kill Avanti," he snarls, his eyes darkening with rage, sliding me off his lap and onto the seat as he stands.

"The guy who my father owed the money to?" I ask, sliding myself back into my own seat next to his.

He freezes and then whips around to stare at me with his brow arched. "Wait. Tell me why you were there last night—exactly."

I scoff. "I think you know exactly why I was there. I had to whore off my virginity to a sick fuck so my father could get the money to pay off his debts and they wouldn't kill us."

I sense a hint of remorse in his expression before it's covered with indignation. "I'm going to ignore that comment about me because I can't say my behavior was gentlemanly last night, but he threatened to kill you?"

"Yes. That's why I did it. I wouldn't have done it to save

my father, but I became a target, or rather a bargaining chip, the second I hit eighteen. Fresh meat, as they like to say." He stares as if he's going to spit venom, but I know it's not directed at me. He's angry about my situation, which makes no sense since he capitalized on it, and if he has his way soon, his investment will bear fruit.

"I will take care of this." He bites his bottom lip and then pulls out his phone, tapping away on the screen before tucking it back in his pocket and sitting down.

"Isn't the threat over? I mean, they got the money, right?"

"Yes, the babaso did," he practically spits.

"Are you regretting giving away that much money for a lousy lay?" He grabs my cheeks a little roughly with one hand. It doesn't hurt, but it has my attention. I'm daring a man who seems to be on the edge, and yet I can't stop myself from pushing.

Staring into my eyes with deadly anger, he snarls, "Don't ever talk about yourself like that again. You are my wife and the mother of my children. I won't allow anyone, including yourself, to demean you. Do you understand, little Dove?"

I nod slightly and then remember to find my voice. "Yes." He lets go as soon as I give him his answer and returns to his computer, typing furiously.

"Are you hungry?" I am, but I'm afraid to eat in front of him. I look down at my body, and I'm still in just his dress shirt. My nipples hardened through the material, which I'm sure he notices. I have on that tiny scrap of panties my father made me wear, but I'm sure my ass cheeks are obscenely sticking out, or at least they would be if I was standing.

"A little. What time is it?" I ask, pulling up the small throw he must have put on me.

"About eight thirty at night." I'm completely lost when it comes to time zones, but the last thing I remember, it was only nine at night. How did I go back in time? Or did I miss an entire day? Ugh. My head can't handle this. I look over at his nearly pristine suit and wonder if he slept at all.

"Oh, goodness. Have you slept?" I'm not sure why I ask, but I do. His face looks a little haggard, but he's still sexy as hell. It should be a sin to look that good and be so damn bad. The dark scruff on his face has gotten a little thicker, and my fingers itch to reach over and rub it.

"No. I only need a few hours a day, and I still have much to do when we land." He seems more annoyed by his busy schedule, like kidnapping me was no big deal.

"You know this is wrong, right? You're kidnapping me," I explain, trying to put up a fight like I'm not his puppet to do with as he pleases.

"Mi pequena, I committed a crime when I paid to fuck away your innocence." My hand comes up before I can think about it, and I slap his face with all my strength. I flinch back, waiting for him to return the favor. He cuffs my wrist and brings it to his face again. This time his mouth parts and his lips kiss my palm. "Forgive me. That was quite rude of me. I will let this one slide because that was crude of me, but if you raise your hand to me again, I will bend you over my knee and spank that pretty little ass of yours and fuck your soaking wet pussy until you cream for me. I will tolerate a lot from you, but I will not tolerate you hurting yourself."

"So, what am I, then? A girlfriend? A—" He presses a finger to my lips, silencing me, and shamefully it works.

"You are my wife, of course."

"Wife? I don't recall a wedding. What was in that drink they gave me?"

"I do not know, but when I find out, I'll have their heads. I'm a proud man, but even I know that what I did to you shouldn't have you passed out for half a day."

"It tasted funny, but I've never had a drink before. My father had strict rules for me, which I'm sure you will too as well."

"That is correct. I will expect you to behave, but I will inform you that you are my wife, and that makes you an equal. When you give our staff an order, they will obey it. Unless it goes against my wishes."

"Of course." I roll my eyes and sit back in my chair, attempting to avoid looking at him again. It's so easy for me to become so captivated by his presence that I forget I'm his prisoner. I want his attention more than I should, craving it like nothing else.

"You are being calm about this," he says with a questioning glare.

"What would you like me to do—scream? Hit you again?" I scoff and then continue. "I have no choice. It's better than going home to what's waiting for me there." As much as I regret revealing that tidbit, it's the truth.

"You are going home. From now on, it's our home," he snaps.

I close my eyes and try to ignore the way he makes me

feel. I'm hungry, afraid, anxious, and despite everything, extremely attracted to Victor. I want to climb back into his lap, but I can't give him another way to control me. I don't have any idea how life will be with him, but I know what it could be if I went home. I've crossed a bridge and burned it to the ground, so there's no return in store. Where do I go from here? Can I escape Victor? Is he a mobster like Avanti?

Will he abuse me if I defy him? He had a chance, but he didn't, although his threat to spank me didn't have the effect he intended. My woman bits clenched up as soon as he warned me. I'm almost tempted to forget myself again just to feel his hand on my ass. Maybe I'm still on whatever drug they put in my drink.

"How long until we arrive?" I ask. I'm not sure if he's told me or not. My mind is practically mush around this arrogant asshole.

He checks the time. "We're about thirty minutes from landing. Do you want something to eat or drink?"

I'm hungry, but we're almost landing. It's not like I'll have time to enjoy my food, and I most definitely don't want to scarf it down in front of him. "Just some water. I'm feeling a little dehydrated." Which is the truth, actually. My mouth is parched.

"Okay." He buzzes the flight attendant, who appears hastily. She looks to be as young as I am and pretty as hell with dark black hair and blue eyes so bright they almost look fake.

"Señor Serrano?" she asks with a nervous smile. "Necesitas algo?" I don't speak Spanish, so I have no idea what they're saying to each other.

"Señora Serrano necesita una botella de agua." She looks to me and then back to Victor with a straight face.

"Si," she says, nodding and walking away and coming back a moment later with a sealed bottle of water. I take it from her and say, "Gracias."

"Gracias, Delia. Es todo." She blushes and walks back the way she came. Oh my God, she's crushing on him, or maybe they have a secret affair and she's blushing because I'm right here so they can't do what they probably always did. A vision of her in his arms runs through my head, and I push that terrible sight out of my mind before I pull her hair out.

"Have you slept with her?" It's out of my mouth before I can bite it back. Gosh, could I sound any more jealous?

"No. She's the pilot's daughter," he says, holding back a chuckle.

"She's nervous around you. I think she has a crush," I finish the last part in a whisper.

"I have that effect on people." His cocky response pisses me off.

"Charming and disarming?" I huff out, and he has the nerve to chuckle.

He reaches out, and I don't flinch as he cups my face, brushing his thumb down my cheek. "No—dangerous. I don't deal in human trafficking, but Avanti and I are not good men."

"I figured as much." Duh. He attended the party with the same intent of every asshole in there.

"Just so you know—if you were anyone else, you'd pay for that remark," he bites out, letting his hand fall.

"I get it. So after I give you an heir, will I be free to go?" I ask.

"Never. Not until they put us in the ground, Dove." There is no hesitation in his response, which makes me wonder why, but I'm too chickenshit to ask anything else. I might not like the answer.

"Wow. Okay."

I ignore him for the rest of the flight until the young attendant returns. "We are about to land. Please buckle up."

Victor nods at her and before I can do it for myself, he's snapping my seat belt into place. "I could have done that myself." He shakes his head with a smirk before fixing his own and relaxing like I didn't just protest. Asshole.

We land, and that's when I notice that we weren't alone the whole time. Three men come from behind me. "Run the sweep."

"Si," the one who's about the same build as Victor answers. Seeing my confusion, Victor stops him from leaving.

"Dove, these men are our personal security. My right-hand man, Fernando."

"Señora Serrano," he says, nodding.

"These two are Julian and Marcelino. They're brothers. I trust them, but I will put this warning out to everyone. Dove is not to be touched unless it's a life or death situation. Dove, you'll never give these men a reason to even put their hands on you. Understood?"

"Por supuesto," Fernando says while the others say yes.

I roll my eyes but agree. "Of course. Although, I think you should know I don't know Spanish."

"You'll learn, eventually."

Again, I roll my eyes and move to leave, but Victor pulls me back. It feels so good to have his hands on me, but it happens so fast that it takes me by surprise. "They need to secure the area before we go," he says, answering the unspoken question in my eyes.

The men leave us while we wait to the side of the door. "Do you have people out to get you too?" The thought of someone coming after him immediately hits me like a ton of bricks. I'm not sure why. It's not even because I like the guy. Maybe it's because I don't want to do without that dick and mouth of his. They're like magic, and his touch makes my body hum.

He takes my hand in his, holding it like we're a couple. "Not exactly, but in my world, most people aren't your friends."

"That's fine. It's not like I have any friends anyway," I grumble.

"Things aren't as bad as you think, Dove." He grazes my chin with his finger, and I want to bite it, to suck on it. I don't know what I want because the man makes me crazy.

"Yeah, says the man who essentially kidnapped me," I say, lashing out.

"You came willingly as I recall. It's not my fault that they slipped you something, which I didn't know until I realized that you slept too long." He does have a point. As far as he knows, I could have just been full of lust and eager to get away from my father. I was eye-fucking him from across the room like the rest of the women in the place.

"Whatever."

His phone buzzes, and he answers it. He's speaking fast in Spanish, so I just ignore it because fuck if I know what he's saying anyway. I failed Spanish in school.

"It's time to go, esposa."

"What does that mean?"

"Wife."

I sigh with a hint of disgust like I don't like it, but that's a lie because my body is alive with desire from just the sound of his voice. He leads me out into the dark of night. I look up and see the stars are beaming. It's beautiful.

"And warmer than New York," I add.

"We do have a slightly warmer climate here. Please be careful." As soon as we hit the last step, I find myself in his arms and I gasp. "I completely forgot about what you're wearing."

"Just your shirt and my panties."

"Yes. I just saw your ass. I refuse to have others see you like this. Your body is for my eyes only."

He helps me into the back seat and then removes his sports coat, placing it over my legs. I look at him like he's crazy.

"There's still a rearview mirror in here." He's serious about anyone seeing parts of me. I don't know how to process all of this.

His phone rings and he answers it, smiling as he speaks to a woman on the other end. I pretend that I'm not bothered or trying to listen, even though I don't understand most of what they're saying. The only thing I pick up is the basic yes and no. Damn it. All my life I've felt alone, and now the painful reality that this will always be my life suddenly feels like more than I can bear.

I turn my head and stare out the window as we pass the city lights and move into farmland, holding back my tears. It's quiet and dark, something I never experienced while in New York. I hated the city because of the hustle and bustle and the money required to enjoy the benefits the city had to offer. I always wished to move out, and here I am. Instead of being happy, I wish for the noise of the city to drown out my thoughts of my fake husband and his plans for making his heir.

I have a million questions, but as soon as he hangs up with one caller, he takes another. Then he shoots off messages. I want to scream and jump out of the moving vehicle, but what good would that do me? I'll have to find a way to escape later. Right now, I'll do my best to be the obedient woman he's hoping for. When the time is right, I'll make a break for it, although I'll need to get a hold of some of his money first. I wonder how hard that will be.

"Planning your escape?" he whispers. I spin so quickly with wide eyes that I'm shocked when he's inches from my face.

"No," I lie.

"Bullshit. I see the wheels spinning in your head. You can leave. Fernando, para por favor." He pulls over on the side of the road. "You can go." He leans over me and opens the door.

"Where can I go? I've nothing but your shirt on my back."

"That's not my problem. Do you want to run out practically naked, or are you going to behave and come along like a good wife?" He's pissed, and I haven't even threatened to leave.

"I'm going with you, aren't I?" I sneer.

He nods and closes the door. "Let's go," he says, tapping Fernando's seat.

He has a self-satisfied smile on his face like he's proved a point. *Asshole.*

He leans in, making me shiver as his breath kisses my neck. "Wife, it's probably for the best that you keep those thoughts to yourself. I might be an asshole, but I'm your husband. I expect you to respect me in front of my men. Comprendes? Understand?"

"Yes," I huff.

"Good." His lips brush my pulse, and my heart picks up its pace. "You may hate me, but your body knows a good thing when it feels it. I can't wait to slip my cock deep inside you again. I have a feeling you want that too." He swipes his tongue up my neck as his hand skims over my thigh. I can't hold back the moan. As soon as I do, he backs off and straightens up.

I do my best to pretend that I'm not offended. I roll my eyes for the thousandth time in the past day and scoff. He grasps my chin hard. "I want you this second, but I refuse to let anyone hear or see your pleasure. You belong to me and me alone." He kisses my cheek and lets go. I turn to face the window to hide my smile.

I may hate him, but I hunger for his hands and body

on me, doing dirty things until I'm screaming for release. My pussy's humming, aching for more. Even when he's rough with me, I'm turned on. There are no words for how aroused I am. Can I be happy with just his orgasms? I don't know. Maybe I'll be able to get a hobby. I'm sure he'll be too busy most days for me and won't give a shit what I do as long as it's not with any other man. That I understand clear as day.

The vehicle slows and then turns to stop in front of a large stone wall and iron gate. There are two men guarding the area, and they open it when they see Fernando. We drive past them with a nod, and the gate slides back in place the second our vehicle passes through.

I'm floored. This home is much larger and grander than Avanti's, and I was completely intimidated by the smaller building. I can't believe this is supposed to be my home. A thought strikes me, and it slips past my lips. "I'll finally have a bed."

"What?"

"Nothing." I pale, hating that I said that loud enough for him to hear.

"That's not fucking nothing. Are you saying that you didn't have a bed at home?" His brows arch while his face hardens.

I blush, feeling completely embarrassed. "Don't be ashamed. You have nothing to be ashamed about." He growls something to himself, and I sense that he's upset for me. Finally, the vehicle comes to a stop in front of the grand entrance. Strangely, a sense of coming home hits me.

5

Victor

THE BASTARD THAT I AM, I've given her no choice—but then again, I did back in the room before I took her virginity. The choice wasn't a real one: life with me, or life being trapped in the grasp of her sick father after giving her pussy to some old married bastard. I had no intention of letting that happen because I would have snatched her up either way, but for some fucking reason, marking her as mine became a must, and my sweet girl wanted it. Her body lit up for me like a Christmas tree. But her father will be dealt with. I will gut that fucker myself.

No one is allowed to do anything to harm my little Dove. Fuck, I hate the way I need her so much. It's blinding and dangerous because my enemies will have a precious new target to aim for, and I refuse to give them an opportunity to strike. Seeing her happy became my mission, but I'm not even sure how to do it after how we met and the fact that I've never wanted to please a woman in this way before. My body aches to carry her back to bed, but it's too soon.

I want to snap at the fact that she's been so fucking deprived that it's a crime. Her father was anything but what a real father should be. At least I had my mother's love to make up for my father's neglect, and we never went without. Where was her mother this whole time?

"Dove, what happened to your mother?"

"When I was six, she fell ill and died of cancer, leaving me with my father who suddenly wanted his freedom, but I was his little burden."

"I'm sorry about your mother." I can't imagine losing my mother. "I'm surprised he didn't toss you in a foster home or something."

"There was money to be had. My mother's life insurance and family inheritance was left to take care of me. He managed to blow through every dollar and then some, and that's how I ended up as a commodity." Fuck, it kills me how much she hates me. How will I ever get her past how we met? Hell, I hate myself for it as well.

"Come, we are home." I take her hand, intertwining our fingers, and lead her out of the back of the SUV. I might not be a known criminal, but I've learned to ride the line often enough and even dip my foot into the cesspool. I'll be burying bodies pretty soon, though. No one gets away with treating my bride like that.

"Wow, this is bigger than the home we met at. Please don't tell me you host parties like that." She drops her chin and narrows her eyes with a look of revulsion.

"I don't host any parties, and especially of such disgusting design. But we will have one to celebrate our marriage here." I lead her to where several of my staff members are waiting to greet us, but I get an uneasy feeling of territoriality so strong that I change my plans. She's hardly dressed for people.

Maria, my housekeeper of six years, approaches. "Señor Serrano, welcome home." She's a good woman, unlike the last housekeeper. When my father died, I brought in an all-new staff, including Maria. I look at the row of staff members and remember that my wife is half naked; instantly a twinge of jealousy stabs me between the eyes.

"Gracias, María. This is my wife, Dove Serrano. You all will address her as Señora Serrano or Mrs. Serrano. Do not disappoint me. We shall be down in the morning. Excuse us." I'm never this terse or abrupt unless there's a major issue that has me running out of the house. I squeeze my wife's hand and lead her past all of them and up the marble stairs. I had planned on introducing her to the head staff members, but then I realize three of them are men and I want to rip their eyes out. Now, all I want to do is mark her with my seed again so everyone knows that she's mine.

I should be giving her a tour of her new home, but it's late and I can't think straight with her body in only my shirt. We enter our bedroom because now I want to forgo everything but owning her body. I release her hand just long enough for her to walk into the center of the room while I lock the door, leaning my back on it while staring at her.

Dove's eyes widen as she takes in our massive California King that I plan to worship her naked body on as often as possible. Sensing my focus on her, she spins, sitting on the edge of the bed, which doesn't help my cause. My dick throbs painfully against the zipper of my slacks. I reach down and adjust myself to relieve the pressure.

"Victor, why are you staring at me like that?" She knows damn well why I'm staring at her and what it means.

"I can stare at my wife any way I please. This is our bedroom where you will most definitely see this look every night."

"Every night?" There's a sexy innocence and yet a hint of playful desire in her words. She bites on her bottom lip gently, making my dick harder than it was. Suddenly, it's not just to prove I own her to the entire house, but because I need her. It will probably pass soon; however, until it does, I'll do all I can to get inside her.

"Dove," I growl, pulling her to me. "I need to be inside you." I can't hide my longing for her. Lust flares in her eyes as I cup her ass and let her feel my raging need. "See what you do to me?"

"The feeling's mutual," she moans.

"We'll see." I reach around and slide my fingers up her thighs, and just like she said, her pussy is soaked for me. She whimpers around my thumb, and I worry that I've hurt her. "Are you okay?"

"It hurts. I need you to make it go away." She shakes as I test her hardened bud. Her body hums under my fingers, demanding more. "Victor, give it to me. I need your touch."

"Always, my little Dove."

I drag my tongue along the smooth skin of her neck, grazing my teeth over her pulse. The way she whimpers in my embrace is the stuff men kill for. I'd kill anyone who dares come between us. Swiping across her flesh and then biting lightly, I feel her heartbeat pick up. "Victor." The little plea goes straight to my balls with precision. My queen needs more. She may hate me, but her body doesn't. I'll use everything I can to tame her until she's as docile as a kitten in my arms. I spin her so her ass presses on my cock and my hands run down her middle, lifting my shirt up her legs, revealing the tiny lace panties that I both hate and love at the same time. "Do you want to come for me, mi reina?"

She nods, and I give her a hard slap on her bare pussy. "I didn't hear you."

"Yes, Victor. I want to come," she hums, laying her head on my shoulder.

"What a good wife." I kiss her neck, sucking and marking her skin because I'm a territorial motherfucker with men eager to take what belongs to me all the time. No one will get their hands on my woman. Never.

I pat her folds, loving the sound her wet cunt makes. The sounds we make could be recorded and made album of the year, but I'd never let anyone hear my queen. That sweet melody is just for me.

"I want you ready for me. I want you so close because I'm going to come the second I'm deep inside of you," I breathe out against the shell of her ear.

"Please." I slip a finger into her just enough to feel her lurch forward and pop her ass back, and then I pull them out and suck her sweetness off my fingers. "Viva la reina,"

I whisper, scooping her up and laying her down on our bed. This is where I should have taken her the first time—devouring her body until she doesn't want to leave and then losing myself deep inside, breeding her, filling her with my heir on our sheets.

I tug at my shirt buttons, hating how long it's taking. Finally able to pull my shirt up over my head, I drop down to kiss her lips. They're soft, plump, eager to feel mine. Her hands slide into my hair, pulling my face closer, moaning as our tongues clash, fighting for our next taste. I have to have more of her honey on my tongue, whipping her pussy into a frenzy before I give her another load. My hand follows my lips as I lick and feel my way to her little slit. It's wet and puffy, waiting for me to give it what it needs. I don't know who's hungrier, but it's my turn to feast. Parting her thighs, I grip her legs and rest them on my shoulders, licking her seam. She moans as I jut my tongue into her wetness, lapping up her cream.

As she shatters and shakes, I rise up and slide into her tight slit, claiming her womb again. I could live inside her sweet depths. I drag myself out and then plunge forward, stretching her. Leaning down, I swipe my tongue across her lips. When she parts them, I thrust it in and deepen the kiss until we're both too worked up, then I trail my mouth along the column of her neck, sucking and nipping on her heated skin. My muscles tense as I start to lose control. "Dove, I need you to come again so I can fill you up with our baby. I want you to cream on my cock. You're going to be a good wife and come, right?"

"Yes," she moans, her nails raking down my back with

a pleasurable sting. I growl and take her in a rough kiss, grinding her into the mattress until she screams my name and then I follow her over. Huffing, I pull out of my wife and roll onto my back, lifting her on top of me.

"Time to sleep, mi epsosa." My heart pounds as I hold her close, breathing in her scent and listening to her as she falls asleep. In the middle of the night, she straddles my hard cock and I lift her up to ride me. Several times we wake up and have sex throughout the night until the sun comes up. I don't know who starts each round, but I make sure to finish them. I need a shower and to get some food in our bellies before I take her again. Maybe I should let her pussy get some rest. I lay there catching my breath, wondering what I should say to her. How can I tell her that this is so much more than sex and a baby? How can I get her to forgive how we met? The sound of my phone breaks through my thoughts.

6

Dove

It's morning as we come down from a fantastic high, lying back catching our breath, panting heavily. I love the way he makes my body sing even though every inch aches. It's tender and completely used up, and yet the man still makes me want more. Victor's the epitome of a virile male with the talent to please sexually. I ignore the reason I'm here and enjoy the pleasure he's giving me.

I'm covered in sweat and a sheet as Victor lies on his back, looking up at the ceiling without saying a word. His phone rings in his jacket on the floor. He's out of the bed and digging it from his pocket to find he missed the call, but he doesn't skip a beat and calls it right back while walking to the bathroom with the phone to his ear as if he wants to make sure I don't hear his conversation. Again.

A couple of minutes later I hear the shower, drilling home my place in his life. I'm his supposed wife so he can have an heir, warming his bed every night and ignoring me the rest of the day. Will we legally get married, or is this just a front? Who was the person who called him?

Who is Victor Serrano?

I know only a few things about the man who has trapped me in his castle of sorts. For one thing, he creates a wall between us the second he pulls out of me. He has some dealings with the wrong kind of people. He got me all the way to Spain without an ounce of trouble. He wants me to have his babies, but he bought me, which probably bothers me more than anything else. Does he usually buy women? Are prostitutes his kick?

He steps out of the bathroom with a towel wrapped around his waist. God, even though he's a total bastard, I can't take my eyes away from his pure sexual being. It pulls me in every time I look at him. As upset I am with him, I'd part my thighs if he asked. Why?

He stares at me with a smirk and then drops his towel. His cock bounces, hard as hell, as if we didn't just have sex. I know he came because I can feel it, but wow. I'm surprised and aroused, and I shouldn't be. "Not right now, mi esposa. Go take a shower. My mother is coming today. You will not tell her how we met, and you will do your best to behave and act like my wife."

I narrow my brows at him, glaring as best as I can before composing myself. With my father, I always kept it under control, but I'm guessing Victor brings it out of me. Standing up, I let the sheet fall as if I don't have a care in the world. With a lift of my chin, I say. "Okay. She doesn't know that you pay for sex?"

I saunter past him, but he quickly grips my bicep and

spins me to face him. His dark eyes return the glare, and he growls with a warning, "If you say that again, I'll keep your ass locked up in here. Are you going to behave?"

"Of course. I don't want to be embarrassed either. I'm sure she'd love that I sold myself to the highest bidder. So, husband, how did we meet? When did we marry?"

He growls again, releasing his grip on my arm. "We met while I was on business, which is true. We married outside the plane before we flew home."

"How am I supposed to lie? We're not married."

"We are most certainly married." He pulls out his phone, opens an app, and shows me my signature on a paper next to his and others. It's a marriage certificate. "See, my wife? Now—my mother is sick, so do not upset her at all. I mean that."

"I'm not mean to most people. I'll save my attitude for those who deserve it. Also, husband, what about some clothes? Did you pick up my belongings before while I was unconscious, or should I wear your shirts?"

"As much as I'd like to see you in just my shirt, that won't do. I ordered clothes for you while we were flying, and my housekeeper had them brought up and put away." He walks over to two double doors and opens them to reveal a large walk-in closet. One side is his suits, and the other is full of women's clothes.

"Are these all for me?" There are so many beautiful things that I don't know how to feel.

"You are my wife. No one else's belongings should be in here. Please try on anything you'd like." I run my fingers over the soft material of the gowns, wondering if he wants his own personal Barbie doll.

"Most of these are too fancy. Or, am I going to have to dress like this all the time?"

"Right now, you're fucking naked, and as sexy as that is, you'll have to wear clothes, so pull open those drawers," he growls, staring at my naked body. His dick jerks under my own perusal of him. "Stop staring at the motherfucker or I'll give you a much closer look," he growls out. How the hell is that so sexy?

I huff and turn my head, pretending to be offended when really I'm tempted to drop to my knees and suck on his huge cock. I open the drawers to my own amazement. There are plain tees and jeans and a drawer of plain white socks. "Oh. Wow." I turn to him, gasp, and look back at the drawer and then back at him.

"I thought you'd like some comfortable clothes as well. I know this is an adjustment, but if there's something you need, please just ask."

I give him a smile, which shocks him. "Thank you. I'll get ready right now."

"You don't have to thank me, Dove. I am your husband and should provide you with these things. I'll finish dressing and wait for you."

"You don't have to wait for me."

"I said I will wait." There's no arguing with him because I already know that he's unmovable.

"Fine." I move past him, brushing my hip against his intentionally.

I'm insanely bold when it comes to him, but somehow, it's because I know I can be. He wants me at his side, but I think it's only until we have babies and then I'll be pushed to the side and become a nanny while he'll keep mistresses galore.

A part of me aches to be bold enough to ask if there's anything other than sex between us, but that's so stupid and naïve of me. *Come on, Dove. Showing your age, aren't you?*

I turn on the shower and let it warm up while I pee and wash my hands. After reading a Cosmo book at the doctor's office, I remember it says to do that after sex so you don't get an infection. I can't imagine he'd be pleased if I got an infection. I hope it's not too late. We passed out after our incredible round of orgasms. I'll give the bastard that. He's an incredible lover. Well, at least until he's done coming. As I look in the mirror, I notice the markings on my pale skin. There are several red spots along with two hickeys. I do my best not to giggle. He's marked me like a teenage boy would his girlfriend. Will he always be so animalistic and territorial?

Get your head out of the clouds and be happy with what you have. A nice warm bed with a sex god and a roof over your head. It's more than I expected out of life less than twelve hours ago. I test the water and it's perfect, so I climb in and sigh as the heat soothes my tender skin.

I see a bunch of female products on the shower rack. It's clear that they're all brand new, which makes me happy. He truly went all out to get this stuff here in time. Did he plan to pick a wife when he left? A virgin sale would be a great place to pick a good girl who hasn't been tainted in his eyes by another man.

Ugh, I bet he's had hundreds of lovers over the years.

Don't go there, girl. You'll only upset yourself and he's not worth it.

I ignore all thoughts of him and wash up quickly. In my rush, I accidentally used his body wash. Oops. Oh well, I'm not going to rewash. I'm sure he's impatiently waiting for me out there.

I tilt my head back and rinse out the conditioner and then rinse my body. I reach out and grab one of the towels and moan against the plush, warm material. These are by far the nicest towels I've ever felt. Damn, things are already a lot better than home. It's not perfect, but I could get used to this—even if I'm trapped in a loveless marriage to a mobster.

I dry my body off in the bathroom so he doesn't see me change. I'm not sure why I'm feeling suddenly self-conscious; the man has seen me naked in every single way, he's tasted my body, possessed it. Once I've slipped on the perfectly fitted clothes, I wrap my hair up again and step back into the bedroom. I'm surprised at the picture in front of me. Victor's not in a suit. I lick my lips, hoping that I get this casual look more often.

7

Victor

I SNARL as the bathroom door closes behind her. Damn it. There should be a rule of no closed bathroom doors. I want to sneak in there and watch her shower. I stab my fingers through my damp hair. I've turned into a little pervert. I'm hard as fuck, thinking about the hot water sliding down her smooth skin. My cock bobs in agreement as I take it in hand. Frustrated, I storm into the closet and pull out a pair of boxer briefs and painfully slip them on over my thick rod. Ignoring the unwanted erection, I pick out a pair of jeans and an undershirt with a pale green polo. When she steps out of the bathroom ten minutes later, I'm floored. She's in a pair of khaki slacks with a light pink fitted polo and bare feet. Her long blonde hair is still wrapped up in a towel with a strand falling out and framing her face.

"Sorry to keep you waiting. I have to brush my hair."

"Take your time. They can wait for us." I sit on the

bed and put on some socks and shoes. The hardwood floors up here are heated, but the rest of the house doesn't have them.

I look up, and she's staring at me. "What's up, esposa?"

"I didn't think you owned jeans," she mutters in surprise.

"I do. I don't wear them often, but we're home and have no plans to go out, so I don't see anything wrong with it." She smiles and then tilts her head toward my cock imprint. Well, that's a setback, but she can make that happen with any pants I'd wear. "Sorry." I'm not sorry. Not one damn bit, especially when her grey eyes flair up with lust.

"You're not really sorry," she says, shaking her head at me with a cute smile, stiffening my dick even more than it is.

"Not when you look eager to feel it inside of you." I cross the distance between us, reaching out and gently cupping her face. The lust in her eyes has my cock leaking onto my boxers. I'm a lost cause, but I don't have time to do what I want to her. "I'm right, si?" I run my hand down her hip slowly.

"You got me," Dove stammers.

I swipe my lips against hers and pull back. "That I do. Finish getting ready. I have a text from my brother. They've just arrived at the gate." I step back and pat her ass.

"Great. Your brother too?" she gasps.

"Yes. And you better not flirt with him. I'd hate to have to kill him."

"Don't sound so jealous."

"I'm not." I'm fucking territorial and insane when it comes to this little one.

"You're not going to greet them?"

"I will when we go down there." She goes to the mirror and begins brushing her long hair. It's not something I ever would have considered sexy, but I can't look away. The brush goes through her golden strands so smoothly that I want to run my fingers through it and then take her, but I have to stop myself and find my voice.

"Okay, you look beautiful. Let's go."

"Am I supposed to go down barefoot?" Fuck me. Every word out of her mouth reminds me of sex.

"Grab a pair of sandals." She goes into the closet and comes out a minute later wearing a pair of cute sandals.

I miss my mother, but I still hadn't expected her to come over so soon. It set me on edge because not only do I want more time alone with Dove, but if my mother knew the truth about our marriage, she would be devastated and so disappointed in me. I already have one woman looking at me like I'm an absolute bastard; I don't need another one, especially after I promised never to be like my father.

I take Dove's hand and lead her downstairs, noticing her fingers are bare. Fuck, I'm screwing this husband thing up every step of the way.

My mother and brother are standing near the steps waiting impatiently for us. Their eyes widen as they get their first glimpse of my wife. "I know I told you to find a wife, but I never expected you to come back with one so quickly, and one so pretty."

Dove blushes beside me. "Mama, my wife, Dove. Dove, my mother, Julia Serrano."

"Mrs. Serrano, it's a pleasure." My mother wraps her arms around Dove and hugs her.

"Am I invisible here?" Hector complains, getting our attention. Dove steps back from my mother and turns her smile on my brother.

"Hello," Dove says, and I'm fucking jealous instantly.

"I'm his little brother, Hector. Mi mama is correct. You are a gem." He wisely doesn't touch my wife but then turns to me and adds, "May I have a word with you, Victor?"

"Will you two ladies excuse us for a moment?" I need to know more about what my mother knows, and I'm sure Hector's ready to grill me. I want this over so I can have Dove all alone and make her cream until she doesn't want to ever leave me.

"Behave, you two. I will keep your wife entertained."

I lean into Dove and whisper in her ear, "Behave, mi amor." Then I kiss her cheek.

We're barely in my office when he says, "You are an idiot."

"Watch it," I growl. If he insults my wife, I'll break his neck.

"Hey, I'm telling you this as a brother who loves you. She's gorgeous and young, but you just made yourself our father."

"I can't let her go."

"Why? Are you worried about what people think?"

"No, because I fucking need her. I knew it the second I saw her. I didn't buy her because I was so hard up for pussy. It's her that I want, and I sure as fuck wasn't going to let someone else there soil her. I almost walked away and then someone put his hands on her, wanting my woman." I stop in my tracks and then screw up my eyebrow. "Wait. How do you know about it?"

"How I know is that as the treasurer, I saw my brother remove that much money and you come back with a wife. It doesn't take much talk to hear you didn't make a deal with Avanti for anything other than that woman," he confesses.

"Who told you?" I want to know how this got out. The thought of people thinking ill of Dove pisses me off. I don't give a fuck what strangers think of me or my motives.

"Mama told me."

My face pales. "Mama?"

"Yes. She overheard some conversation while out shopping about your request for a full feminine wardrobe and everything in the house. She knows you met with guys like us, like Father. She put it together herself."

"She thinks so little of me." I sigh, falling back on my leather sofa, laying my head over the arm.

"No, she hopes not, but we know you're not like Father. Still, how does this girl feel about this?"

"My wife's not in love with me if that's what you mean, but she doesn't resist my touch. She loves it."

"So she's attracted to you. That's good."

"But she'll never love me." Wow, I sound fucking weak as hell. What happened to me?

"Whoa. You're already in love with her, aren't you?"

"Of course I am. There's no other reason I'd do what I did."

"Then show her. Maybe she'll come to love you. It's only been a day. Fuck, has it even been a day?"

"No. It hasn't. I moved mountains to make her mine, and now I've trapped her just like our mother was."

"Just prove you're not our father."

"Wait. Mom knows." Fear drains all the color from my face. Will she help Dove leave me?

We storm out of the room and go in search of them. Vicente points to the kitchen. I swing the door open and accidentally hit my wife. "Shit. Dove." I catch her before she hits the ground. "Amor, are you okay? I'm sorry."

"I'm fine," she says, moving out of my arms.

"We were just making some lunch. Since when don't you know how to open doors, Victor Miguel?"

"Oh shit. She used your middle name." Hector laughs.

"You're next. Are you well, mija?" She cradles my wife's shoulders.

"I am." Suddenly her stomach grumbles loud enough for us to hear.

"Starving your wife?" My mother tsks, wagging her finger at me. She takes Dove and brings her to the kitchen island and hands her some chopped apples. "Eat these while I finish the food."

"We have a cook, Mama," I remind her as I move close to my wife.

"I know, but I like my cooking. Besides, I have him running to the store for us."

"Victor is correct, Mother. You should be resting," Hector says, putting his arm around her.

She nudges his arm away as she works on making tortillas de patatas. "Dejame. I'm fine. Now, either sit and behave, or leave us." Both of us look at her, feeling like little boys again, which makes Dove smile. Fuck me, she's gorgeous. I'm so fucking lost, it's pathetic. I have an empire to run.

Just then, my phone rings. "Serrano."

"You kidnapped my daughter."

I cover the phone. "Hector, come with me. I'll be back." I bend down and kiss Dove's lips. Then she raises an apple slice for me.

Seeing my surprise, she says, "You didn't eat either." I bite down on it and smile before walking out of the kitchen.

"Watch them. No one goes in there," I tell Vicente.

"Understood."

As soon as I'm in my office and Hector has the door closed, I put the prick on speaker.

"So who the fuck are you?" I hiss out.

"I told you who I am!" he roars, like I should be intimidated by that weak bastard.

"No, you didn't. I don't know who your daughter is, but I didn't kidnap anyone."

"You lying, rich sack of shit. My daughter deserves better than you, you Spanish scum."

"I will speak with you when you learn some manners, pinche babaso."

I end the call. I will not tolerate being spoken to like that. He already has a death sentence headed his way.

Now he's made it a slow and painful one. "He's a dead man walking."

"Who the hell is that?"

"I presume it's Dove's father—the son of a bitch who put her up for sale to Avanti in the first place."

"What are you going to do?"

"I'm going to put a bullet in his head in good time. I have to play it smart, but after what he's done to her, there's no way he's getting anything less than a death sentence."

"Please tell me he didn't..."

"No. Of course not. It's not like he could sell her for so much money if he did. That asshole Avanti is on my list too. The money Falcone owed was to Avanti himself. He knew that and laughed in my face. If I'd known at that moment, I might have shot him between the eyes." I still might. He sold my woman and disrespected me multiple times. The fact that Falcone got my number tells me all I need to know about Avanti. He's a dead man.

"He'll pay, brother. We'll make them all pay. She seems sweet—too sweet for you."

"She is. I don't know much about her, but she's strong. Her temper will get her into trouble with me, but I've got the feeling she'd love my hand on her ass. I know I can't wait for her to act up."

"Oh shit, bro. Didn't know you had that kinky shit going on." He laughs, then claps my shoulder. "Oh wait. I hope that didn't turn you on?"

"Fuck off. She's changed me in ways I never expected. I don't know how I'll ever make her fall in love with me when now I'm sure as fuck that I'm in love with her."

"Get to know her. Give her some freedom. Talk to her. You're not an asshole all the time."

"I suppose I could give it a shot. I don't know about the freedom, but I'll see if there's anything she's interested in and get it for her. Maybe she likes to draw, paint, or binge watch television."

"Netflix is the way to go with that."

"I'll keep that in mind." Now to get rid of my guests and find Dove so I can spend the day getting to learn about my wife.

"Everything okay?" Dove asks after swallowing a bite of her food. I come up to her and pull her into my arms and kiss her.

"Yes. Now, Mama. I am starving." I rub my hands together and pull up a seat next to Dove. My mother sets a plate for both of us boys. "Gracias."

"So I'm going to have Hector take me home in a bit, but I just had to meet your wife."

We dine, and then my mother takes my brother by the arm and drags him out. "I'm not even done, Mama."

"I'll make you more later. Come. They have a baby to make."

Dove coughs, nearly choking on her food. "I'm sorry. Are you well?"

"Yes. Sorry, she made me laugh."

"Sorry about her. She's very insistent when it comes to grandbabies."

"Well, she may get her wish soon, I suppose." She's staring at me again, biting on her bottom lip.

"Are you looking for another round, Dove?"

"I don't know what you mean." She's playing coy, but

she hasn't stopped looking at my cock since they walked out.

"We will take a tour of the house after I reacquaint you with our bed." I scoop her up in my arms and flip her over my shoulder. "Then maybe you'll stop ogling my dick."

"Stop making it so damn prominent, and then I won't."

"You're the one making me hard. I can't get enough of being inside that tight, warm pussy of yours," I growl, taking the stairs two at a time.

"Everyone can see us."

"Well, they know the boss has plans for his wife, then, and they'll not interrupt me." She has no idea how tempted I was to fuck her right there in the kitchen, but I was too afraid of someone walking in and I'd have to kill them for seeing my wife in the throes of passion.

The second we're in our bedroom, I stalk toward the bed, tossing her on it. "Lose the clothes, wife. I want your pussy on my tongue in less than a minute." She smiles and lifts her blouse off over her head. Her light pink bra is a little too small, and her tits are about to spill over. "I'm going to have to order you a larger size, no?"

"Yes, but this one is so cute." It is for sure. I drop my head and forget about our minute because I can't wait. Dragging the cup down, I suck on her soft breast, feeling her peak stiffen in my mouth, and lave my tongue in circles around her pink, puckered nipple until it's completely hard and then I move to the other. She reaches between us and undoes my belt. I manage to get control of myself long enough to get her capris down her legs. Nudging her panties to the side, I slam inside her warmth.

"I can't wait anymore." Grunting and pumping, I lift up one of her legs onto my shoulder as she lays on the edge of the bed, taking every inch of me. I can't get enough of her to stop. I bend down and take her mouth, kissing her like I'm starved. I want her to the point of pain. "I need to come, Dove. You're going to come for me, aren't you? Your soaking wet pussy's greedy and wants my cum, doesn't she?"

"Yes, give it to me, Victor. I need to come," she breathes out between kisses. Sweating from teetering on the edge of my release, I stroke her little nub. Her eyes close, body tenses, back arches, and her voice cracks as she cries out my name, squeezing every drop of cum out of my sack and into her womb. Letting go of her leg, I lift her around the waist and pull her onto the bed completely.

"Fuck, you're so damn sexy when you come on my cock," I growl, leaning over her with my hands on the bed, and kiss my wife.

My phone buzzes in my pocket, and I wish I didn't have to bother with the damn thing. "Excuse me." Pulling out of her heat always feels like fucking torture.

"Of course." I can tell she's upset that I've gone for my phone again, but I'm a busy man and it's why I haven't gotten laid in many damn years. I don't have time for a wife, and I wasn't expecting Dove. I hate every call that comes to drag me away from home, especially now that she's all I want.

"What is it, Fernando?"

"Someone has caused damage at the vineyard. They set it ablaze. They are putting it out now, but the policia are here with questions."

"I'm on my way."

I hit the shower and do a quick wash up. I'd go wearing her scent anywhere, but I'm fucking nuts and I don't want anyone to know what she smells like when she comes for me. I'd rip their throats out for breathing in her release, even if it's all I want to smell. As soon as I wrap a towel around my waist, I turn on the bathtub for her. I'm sure her pussy must ache. My dick has felt the brunt of her innocence, but I'll deal with the pain just fine as long as I get to have her warmth over and over again.

I step out into the bedroom and she's sitting on the bed looking thoroughly fucked, but her mind's elsewhere to the point she doesn't acknowledge my entry back into our room. There's a sense of disappointment that I don't have her attention. In less than a day, I've grown addicted to having her grey eyes on me, appraising me in one way or another. My phone buzzes again from the bathroom, so I grab it and then head into our walk-in closet and dress in a suit. I'm fixing my cuffs when I call out her name.

"Dove." She finally turns to look up at me.

"Sorry. I was lost in thought."

"I've run you a bath. I'm sure you have to be sore." I walk over to her and taste her lips. "I want you nice and relaxed." I walk away and turn off the water.

8

Dove

"I have to leave and handle some business. I'll be back around five," he says, adjusting the cuffs on his white dress shirt. After our second morning jaunt in the sack, he quickly gets up to shower, like I didn't expect that already. I watch him get ready, and I'm a little taken aback about the way he carries himself.

He looks sexy both in and out of business attire, but I'm truly partial to the whole suit thing. The fact that he gets to leave looking that good raises my hackles. I hate how jealousy invades my soul when it comes to this man. We haven't even been here a full twelve hours, and he's leaving already. I look at the large clock in our bedroom, and it's merely ten.

"Okay." I'm not trying to come off as petulant, but my emotions are getting the better of me.

"Is there anything you like to do for fun?" he asks.

"I usually run, but since I'm sure you're not going to let me out of the house, I read."

"Don't sound so miserable. There's a gym in the house and a treadmill if you really want to run and are not just trying to bust my balls. We have a library. It doesn't have any contemporary romance novels, but it does have the classic ones if that's what you want to read. I can get you one of those reading devices if you want and you can select books to order online."

"Do you all have a bookstore nearby?"

"There are bookshops in Madrid, but most of the literature is in Spanish."

"Oh. I forget that I'm not home." I sigh heavily. I could really use a Barnes and Noble.

"This is your home," he snarls. Goodness, he really hates when I say that.

"I meant in New York where Spanish is the second language."

"So if it's the second one, how come you never picked it up?" It's a fair question, I suppose.

"I failed it in school. I hated my Spanish teacher. He was a grade-A prick who thought my eyes were located on my chest."

"Oh. Okay."

"What does that mean?"

"Nothing. I'll have a Kindle for you when I return, and then you can order whatever books you'd like."

"Even how to dispose of a dead body?" I challenge, thinking I'm funny.

He closes the distance and then slides his hand into my hair and pulls me close so his breath tickles my neck and then says, "Then you could help me, but the books don't really do it justice." He kisses my lips and walks out of the bedroom door. I shake my head and smile, pressing my hand to feel the heat and electricity. Then, the door pops open and Victor sticks his head back in. "Remember what I said about anyone touching you."

I nod. "Okay."

I walk into the bathroom and still smell his body wash. I hate how much I crave his smell. I look over the latest marking and frown. I can't look at the possessive marks when he seems quick to fuck and run. I take my sour mood and push it away. He ran a nice hot bath for me, and I have the house to myself. What is there really to complain about? What would my life be like if I was forced to the streets if I escaped my father's grasp?

I laugh to myself as I slide into the bath. A moan escapes my lips as the heat feels great on my aching body. I've never been in a bathtub this large. I probably will never get out. I lay my head back and think about my father. What must he be thinking now? Is he freaking out? Missing out on another payday with me? I'm sure he's pissed that his only asset was snatched away.

Snatched away by a wicked Spaniard with a need to devour every inch of me. It's hard to stop being turned on by Victor. He left, and I'm still aroused. I need to find a hobby. I wonder how massive his library is. Is it Beauty-and-the-Beast massive, or barely a study's space worth of books? In this day and age, most people don't have physical books. I love having actual books in my hand, but I'll settle for whatever I can get. Finally getting out of the tub when I'm chilled and my fingers and toes are wrinkled, I wash off the bubbles and wrap a massive towel around my body. Feeling the exhaustion of everything, I fall onto the bed and pass out.

I wake up, and the sun is bright in the sky. Looking over at the clock, I see it's already one thirty, and my stomach rumbles. I do the math on my fingers. I passed out for two hours. Strange. There's a blanket covering me. I don't remember pulling it over me. I stretch out and feel the ache through every part of my body. Well, I better get dressed and look for some food, and then I need to find this library. I slip on panties and a bra, then dig out a plain white T-shirt and a pair of green khaki shorts from the drawer. My hair's a little curly from falling asleep with it wet, so I brush it and put it in a long braid. I'm so grateful whoever brought the clothes and supplies remembered basic hair ties. I slide on a pair of almost generic flip-flops.

As soon as I step outside my door, I'm surprised when I nearly collide with a guard. "Oh my goodness. Sorry." All the while, my mind is racing about why Victor has someone keeping tabs on me.

"I'm the one who's sorry. I'm Vicente. I normally guard around the house. I just spoke to the boss, and he's gone for the day. Do you need anything?"

"I'm actually heading down to the kitchen." I remember where that is because it's the one place I've actually spent time in other than our bedroom since I arrived.

He nods and continues to patrol the corridor before coming down the stairs. I hear him say "all clear" into his earpiece.

I don't know why they would do a check upstairs when no one got in or out of the house, but whatever. I'm new to this world, even though it's how we met. My father was mafia adjacent, an errand boy of sorts, but that's all I know about the life.

Frankly, I have no idea what Victor does or how dark his story is, and I don't want to know. I'm not sure I could handle the details.

When I get to the kitchen, his housekeeper, Maria, is in there with the cook, whom I haven't met yet.

"Good afternoon, Mrs. Serrano. How are you?"

"I'm starving, actually."

"Oh, no. Let us get to it."

"No, it's okay. I can make my own food."

"Señor Serrano left strict instructions that I'm to prepare your meals. I am Geraldo, by the way. I am the chef around here."

"So do all of you live in the house?"

"There are several employee homes on the estate. There are the old servants' quarters that Señor Serrano keeps for the staff who have to stay overnight or work long days, but the rest of the mansion is for his family. Dona Serrano and Hector have their own rooms, but they rarely stay."

"We can't wait until there are little ones running around here."

"How long have you been working for Victor, if you don't mind me asking?"

"You can ask any question you like. I actually worked for the winery's restaurant when Señor Serrano's father died. He was looking for a new housekeeper and offered to give me the job. I have been here six years now."

"I've only been here for five years after working in France for a decade."

"Wow. France? I've never been there. Hell, I hadn't left New York until Victor scooped me up and brought me here." My stomach rumbles loud enough to gather everyone's attention.

"Let me feed you before it's the end of my five years. What would you like?"

"Something simple. I don't know if Victor's going to be home in time for dinner. I don't know how you all operate over here."

"Dinner, as you'd say back in America, will be around seven, assuming there is no change in plans. Señor Serrano is extremely easy to please when it comes to his foods. What do you like?"

"Not to starve. A salad or sandwich would be good. Breakfast was delicious, but I've hardly eaten in the past couple of days, so I couldn't eat that much."

"Will a pork sandwich hold you over until dinner?"

"Yes, please. I'm not a picky eater, but I'm not accustomed to the food here."

"You'll get used to it. Tell us if you don't like a dish I make or if you do, and that way I'll be able to feed you. Also, I have traveled over my lifetime and learned many American and Mexican dishes if you choose to have something from your old home."

"Thank you." For the next twenty minutes, Geraldo

tells me about the places he's been while Maria makes a list of things I like. So far, the staff has been excellent and this pork bocadillo is fantastic. By the time we're done chatting and eating, I decide to head over to the library somewhere in this big house.

"I'm going to run and pick up the things on this list that we don't have."

Do you need anything?" Maria asks.

"I think I am fine. You supplied me with everything so far. I can't ask for more."

"Que preciosa. You are too precious. We are here to serve you. If you need anything, please do ask. Señor Serrano would be quite upset if he learned you weren't being taken care of."

"Thank you. If I do think of anything, I will let you know. I'm off to the library now. Thank you for lunch and the chat." I walk out of the kitchen and nearly bump into Vicente again. "We have to stop meeting like this," I say playfully. He's older than me, but not much older. He's dressed like the others, but there's something about him that screams arrogant. Maybe it's the way he carries himself. Either way, it's none of my concern because Victor knows who he has working for him.

"I'm sorry, Mrs. Serrano."

"It's okay. I'm off to the library, so beware. Oh, and by the way, which way is it?"

"I'll escort you there." He leads the way, making sure to keep his distance. I feel an awkward silence that unsettles me, so I make some small talk as he leads me down the long corridor off the kitchen.

"It's sad that I'm lost around here, but I'll get the hang of it."

"Yes, we can't have you getting lost forever." He gives me a nervous smile that brings my own grin to my face.

"Here we are." He waves his arms at the large wooden doors.

"Thank you. I don't know how long I'll be in here, so you don't have to follow me anymore. It's not like I'm going anywhere."

"Just doing my job."

"Well, I don't want to be disturbed." It may come off rude, but seriously, I'm a little annoyed that he's up my ass. I know Victor doesn't trust me, and that's why he has his minions following me like puppies. Still, I find it irritating.

"Call out if you need anything." He nods and turns on his heel in the opposite direction we came from. This house is practically a castle. It definitely has that historic charm. I open the double doors like I'm in Beauty and the Beast and to my amazement, the library is massive. Two floors with a walking path on the second. It's beautiful. I close the door behind me and then walk to the nearest bookcase and run my fingers along the spines of the books while breathing in the scent of paper. A happy sigh escapes my lips, and then I scan the titles. There are so many titles that I'm not sure which one to pick.

I randomly grab a small stack and sit on the most comfortable chaise ever. It's heavenly.

I pick up the first book. It's *A Tale of Two Cities*, which I immediately put down. The next is Thomas Paine's *Common Sense*. This time, I read at least a page before setting it on the table beside the head of the chaise. Next is *Dracula* by Bram Stoker. Unable to stop myself, I dig in. Page by page, I devour the story until there's a knock at the library door.

"Yes?"

"Señor Serrano has pulled into the driveway."

"Thank you." I don't care. I look at the clock on the wall, and it's already six thirty. I grumble the time to myself and go back to my book. I refuse to look up when he enters the library.

"If that's the greeting I get when you're engaged in reading, I'll just have to take this back to the store."

"You're late," I hiss, refusing to look up from the book.

"Oh...well. I was busy working." I turn and look at him, and he's wearing a different shirt.

"Working? Why is your shirt different?" I question, narrowing my eyes so he knows damn well I'm not stupid.

"I spilled wine on it."

"Oh, work. Wine?"

"Dove, we own a winery," he says.

"A winery?" Well, I didn't know that.

"Yes. An entire vineyard as well. I'll take you one day if you'd like."

"That sounds good." I stare at him and wonder why he had wine and why he spilled it on himself. "Do you keep extra clothes just lying around?"

"If I didn't know better, I'd say you were jealous."

"Not in the least. I'm just curious."

"I do, actually. I hadn't planned on getting dirty, but sometimes that comes with the business." I don't know which business he's actually referring to, and I'm not going to ask. "So anyway, wife. Any more questions, or can I give you your tablet?"

"You got it for me?" I gasp, shocked by it.

"Of course I did. I couldn't get you a Kindle, although I can order you one from Amazon, but I was told you can download the app on here and it works the same." He hands me a Samsung Tab A. "Oh, and you'll need this to go with it." He hands me the latest Samsung, or at least I think it is. I don't know about phones other than the multitude of ads I saw on the bus in the city or on the TV sometimes. I used to have the first Samsung Galaxy they ever made, or at least it felt that way.

"Thank you! I've never had a new phone or a tablet before." I throw my arms around him again today for spoiling me. We might not have a real marriage made from love, but he's not doing a bad job on some of the aspects of being a husband. It's better than being trapped doing nothing. At least I think I can play games on this thing.

"That's much better. I have to leave again, but I will be back around midnight. I picked this up at the store. You can use it to order your books." It's a hundred-dollar Amazon gift card. Wow. "Let me know if you need more. I can set up an account. I'll be back." He takes my lips fast and hard before rushing back out of the room.

I forgot to ask him about the phone. Then he comes back in. "Oh and there's no point in calling the cops. They won't come here to get you, okay?" His mouth is on mine once more before leaving. Damn, I hadn't even thought about the cops. I set everything down and go back to my book. I guess I'll be having dinner on my own while he's out doing God knows what and with who. I don't think he's cheating. He's gone through too much trouble and he's fucked me way too many times in the past twenty-four hours to need his dick hard again.

I sit on the chaise and continue my book until there's a knock at the door half an hour later. "Mrs. Serrano, I'm sorry, but dinner is ready. Would you like it served here, in the dining room, or in the kitchen?"

"The kitchen, if you don't mind."

"This is your home."

"I have to remember that." They have been so nice to me. "I'm coming now." I take my book and my new gadgets and carry them with me into the kitchen.

9

Victor

I've been out of the house all day, dealing with the new family out there. I couldn't believe it when I learned who it was. Julio Montoya had the balls to finally go up against me, but what he doesn't understand is that I have more to lose now than ever, and that means I have something to fight for. I'll fight to the motherfucking death to protect my Dove.

I can't prove who set the blaze in my damn vineyard. There are many dirt roads with access to the vineyards. We can't have it locked up because it brings in the tourists, but now it's allowed the rats to enter. With a wife and hopefully a baby on the way, I don't want a war, but they've pushed me to the point I must make a decision. A quarter of my vineyard burned to ashes in broad daylight means someone's going to get their heads lobbed off.

I spent the morning working to evaluate all that we lost. When I finally checked the time, I realized I was fucking late as hell. Fernando rushed me to the store to get Dove's present. Seeing her jealousy pissed me off. She can call it whatever she wants, but she thought I was out fucking another woman and came home with a different change of clothes. What she doesn't understand is there could be no one else. I only see her now, and nothing will change that. It's not love or respect that gets her to distrust me. It's our lack of it that makes her think that I have nothing else on my mind. I bought her like a prostitute, after all.

When I handed her the phone, I nearly caved, but I have to have a way to get in touch with her and vice versa. I don't want her to ever think she can't call me. My number and Fernando's are the only ones programmed into the phone because I want her to be able to call me whenever.

Damn it. I should have told her that. "Have you heard any movement on the Vitalis' end?"

"None. I contacted the businesses nearest the entry to the vineyard for any footage."

"We need to install cameras up and down on all the telecommunication poles."

"Nothing flashy and nothing that's going to grab people's attention. I don't want it to look like the surveillance at the house."

My phone rings, and it's my half sister Maria Luisa. "Are you still coming to your godson's party?"

"Yes."

"Are you going to bring your lady friend?"

"No. How did you hear about her?"

"I thought it was idle gossip. I didn't believe it. I can't

believe it. I'm so happy for you. I want to meet her one day, but I won't push."

"One day, I will introduce you two. So who told you?"

"We're women. Word spreads quick. Mi amiga works next to the store and heard about a large delivery and how the owner was worked up about getting it right."

"Well, I will say this. I can't go without an heir forever."

"Good. I'm so happy for you. Take care of yourself. Treat her right."

"I will. Take care as well." I end the call.

"I'm ready to go home. I think we've done enough for the night."

"Sounds good. I need a fucking shower and some food."

"You should have eaten with the guys."

"Nah. I didn't want that shit. I was hoping for Geraldo's famous caldo."

"I'm sure there's a lot left. There's only Dove eating. Shit. I didn't ask if she's allergic to anything. Damn it. I'm fucking this all up."

"I don't know about all that shit, but I say we cap her father and Avanti soon so she has nowhere to run to. You gave her a phone. I wouldn't have."

"She can't make international calls on it."

"There's still internet on it, right?"

"Yes."

"Then she can Facebook call or use any of the apps that allow you to call internationally."

"Shit. Son of a bitch."

"I'm not saying she's going to, but just be careful. Do you want me to track her keystrokes on the tablet?"

"I shouldn't, but go ahead."

"At least until you're sure she's not going to run."

"Do you think I'm a fool?"

"Not at all. I'd just hate to see if she tried to leave you."

"Let's drop this shit." We pull through the gate and Fernando drops me off at the front steps while he parks. It's already one in the morning. Fuck, she's got to be passed out now.

I enter the house, hoping to be quiet. My stomach rumbles, but I just want to see my wife. When I push open the bedroom door, she's not inside. I call out her name but I get no answer, so I check the bathroom and it's empty.

Running down the stairs two at a time, Fernando sees me and I bark out, "She's not up there." I storm through the house, looking for my guards, but I didn't tell them to keep an eye on her partly because I'm a jealous son of a bitch, but because it wasn't like she could leave. The outside is a fortress. They won't let her out by herself.

I open the library door and there she is, sleeping with a book on her chest. My heart's beating against my ribs, and I release a sigh. Fernando's footsteps stop at the door. "I'll be in the kitchen. Do you want some food?"

"Yeah." I grab the throw over the back of the other chair and lay it over her. I'll get her after I eat.

A half hour later, I can't wait any longer to see my Dove. I enter the library, and I see the tablet on the table next to her head. I touch it, and the first thing I see is her internet browser open. They say you shouldn't snoop just in case you don't like what you see, but I can't stop myself. *Divorce in Spain for non-citizen. International abduction. How to cross borders without documents.*

I slam it down and step on it. This startles her awake. "Victor?"

"Yes, it's your husband, wife."

"What happened?"

"Your tablet was on the floor. I accidentally stepped on it."

"What? It was still in the box." I look, and the box is sitting on the table.

"Maybe you didn't remember to put it back."

"I didn't even turn it on. I've been reading this." She shows me *Frankenstein*, which is open halfway. "I read *Dracula* earlier and wanted to read another gothic book. What time is it?" She's fucking lying to me. I hate it. I want to grab her around the throat and tell her she's staying put, and if she lies to me again I'll punish her good, but I don't want her running from me.

"It's almost two. Come—it's time for bed."

"Did you just get back?"

"No. I ate dinner. Come. It's time for bed. Don't make me tell you again."

"Look, you don't have to be a prick." She throws off the blanket and stands, pushing away my proffered hand. She marches past me, leaving her phone and book lying there. I take her phone with me to examine later. Fernando was right. I shouldn't have given her that much trust.

I follow behind her, nearly catching the bedroom

door in the face as she attempts to slam it behind her. She strips out of her shorts and then walks into the bathroom. This is going to be a fucking nightmare.

I strip down and wait for her to get out of the bathroom before I go in there to get ready. Once I come back out, she's on her side, sleeping or at least pretending to sleep. I turn off the lights and climb into bed beside her.

10

Dove

It's been three weeks since he brought me here, and in that time, we've spent our nights together in bed. He hardly speaks to me most days. So, we're going to play this game, as if we're really married. My heart thumps in my chest every time Victor's hands are on me, but it must be a sense of revulsion. I do my best to avoid his touch, but he's not shy about taking what he wants, even down to the subtle caresses.

Night after night we fuck like lust-filled lovers, but then he's gone in the morning as if I'm nothing but a nightly stop off. It breaks my heart. Everyone around here treats me like a queen, meeting every need I have, but it's Victor I want, and not just his impressive dick. I want his love—something I'm afraid I'll never have. Maybe it's my naivety that allows me to hope, but day after lonely day, that feeling fades more and more.

Today, I'm breaking his rules and sneaking out. I've

had enough of being just here. Victor has a meeting today in another part of the country, which means he can't get to me that fast once he finds I've stolen his credit card.

Whatever. All I care about is getting out of the house. I spend most of my days alone in our bedroom or in the library. They bring me my food because I keep forgetting to eat, which seems to work Victor's nerves. He spanks, then fucks me when I forget. I'm starting to enjoy my sudden forgetfulness. Although that's the extent of our relationship. We've never moved past the sexual aspect of our relationship. Hell, he still hasn't even given me the tour he promised me.

Victor enters our bedroom when I thought he was already leaving. "Don't you look adorable. Where do you think you're going?"

"Since when do I go anywhere? Not that you would have noticed. You would have to be here to notice that. So anyways, I'll be lounging about while attempting to wear some of the more fashionable pieces you bought."

"I can ask my mother if she wants to come over."

"Thanks, but no thanks. I don't want to hear more talk about babies and all of the things we can do to the nursery."

"Someone's in a bad mood. I'll be home by this evening. Are you going to be in a better mood then?"

"I don't know. Maybe it's that time of month, so who knows."

"Is it?"

"I don't know. I've lost track of my schedule."

"Well, if it is, please let me know."

"Don't worry. You'll be notified."

"Okay. I really have to go or I'll be late."

"I'm not stopping you." I hold back the tears. I'm losing my heart to a man who only has one use for me.

"Damn it, wife."

"I'm fucking bored. You leave, and I'm stuck here. You never replaced my tablet; my phone is limited to phone calls now. You're treating me like a prisoner, not a wife, so don't call me your wife."

"You're my fucking wife no matter how much you don't want to be here. I don't give a fuck how bored you are. Maybe you'll learn not to fucking lie to me."

"I've never lied to you." Okay, I never lied before. Now I'm furious with him. He's an asshole who thinks sex is going to keep me here.

"Don't start that shit. I won't let my guard down again."

"I thought you said you have to leave."

"Don't get smart with me. I have to go, but if you misbehave, I'll make sure you'll be punished."

"Misbehave? Like tell your employees that we're not in love and that you paid to have me?" He's on me in a second with his hand wrapped around my throat and his thumb pressing my chin upward.

"You like to test me, don't you, my little Dove?" He gives a tiny squeeze. It's not to hurt me, but to show he's serious. All it does is cause my pussy to gush cream all over my panties. He's so damn hot when he's bossy. "You do, because you know I'm going to have to remind you that you're mine, but today I do not have time. You will have to wait for your punishment. Behave."

"I'm going to behave. It's not like I need everyone to know my shameful past." He growls and releases his grip.

After twenty minutes, there's a knock at my door. "Señora Serrano, are you ready?"

"I'm coming."

I walk to the door and open it up. Vicente stands there in a suit like the rest, but he's looking a little less stiff. He gives me a smile that makes me smile back. Of all the guards here, he's been the nicest to me. The rest are super stiff and just answer my questions with as few words as possible. Lately, everyone has been a little colder except Vicente, Maria, and Geraldo.

"Looking lovely, Dove. We better head out before the shops get crowded." I'm shocked by his informality, but I'm just excited to get out of the house so I don't press it. He offered to take me when I mentioned sneaking out as a joke. Still, I don't like his informality. That's the first time since I arrived that anyone other than Victor has called me by my name instead of Señora or Mrs. Serrano.

Fernando and two other guards are going with Victor today. Vicente is supposed to be at the gate, but right now there's no one there and we have time to sneak out. I've already made up a lie so Vicente doesn't get into trouble.

We move to his black sedan, and he opens the front passenger door. "I figured you'd want a little less formality today."

"Thanks," I say, turning my head with a smile. I really do want to not feel trapped or scared. He helps me in with his hand on my side, and I freeze. No one is allowed to touch me. Damn it, I hope he doesn't get in trouble for it. Maybe no one saw it. I close my eyes and then buckle my seat belt as he shuts the door.

Once he goes around and enters, I say, "You shouldn't touch me. It's one of Victor's rules."

"Honest mistake. It is customary as gentlemen." He gives me a half smile.

"Yes, but I don't want Victor to take it out on you. He's a little crazy, and I'm already pushing the envelope today."

"It shall be our secret." He winks and then begins to drive. I'm getting a strange vibe about all of this. Maybe it's because I'm not used to people being nice to me or because I know that I'm in for it when I get back.

"So how far is it from here?"

"About ten minutes. Relax. It's your first day of freedom. There are a lot of stores for you to enjoy. Street vendors are out and about. Do you have anything like that in New York?"

"Yes, lots of them. Does it get that busy here?" What if there's one of Victor's enemies out there waiting for the right moment to strike? I know he's done a good job of hiding our marriage. I don't even have a ring on my finger.

"Not at all."

"Good. Are you going to be my translator?"

"Yes, little Dove." Okay. That sends a chill through me, and I don't say another word. Victor would be angry at the familiarity. I'm uncomfortable with it.

"Is something wrong?" he asks as he comes to a stop.

"I would just prefer if we keep this less friendly. Victor wouldn't be happy."

"I'm surprised you care. Unless you're just worried about being killed by him, then I'd understand. He's a ruthless son of a bitch. He keeps you trapped while out banging his mistress every week. It's where he's going on 'business' today. He always goes to see her and their two daughters."

"What?" I gasp, nearly choking on my own shock.

"I'm just saying. It makes no sense that he brought you here and married you when he has a ready-made family." He shrugs like this is no big deal and that I'm already aware of Victor's betrayal.

He barely finishes parking when I get out of the car before he can stop me. I don't want to hear more right now and sadly, I don't want to believe him because my heart can't handle the betrayal. It's silly because I'm just another possession to Victor, but I still hurt.

Taking a deep breath, a plan comes to my mind. I am going to spend Victor's money like it's going out of style, and then I'm going to resell the shit and get a ticket out of my own personal hell.

"Are you okay, Dove?"

"I'm fine. I'm here to shop. Please, no more talk of my fake-ass husband." He follows behind me—a little too close for comfort per Victor's request, but my chest is too busy breaking. We go from store to store, most staring at me in wonder especially when we pay. I might have stolen Victor's card, but he stole my heart and then broke it. If he's going to treat me like a whore, I'm collecting on the tab.

11

Victor

THREE WEEKS, and things aren't getting better. If anything, they've gotten a shitload worse. Dove has only let me into her body. Her heart remains unavailable to me. It's as if she's hardened it so hard that I may never get her to love me. Perhaps I haven't given her a reason.

"Did you pick up the gift like I asked?" I inquire, knowing it's pointless because he wouldn't forget. He's not the one with his head up his ass. I'm the one with a wife who takes up every thought in my head, causing me to be careless. I should have handled the little attacks by Julio's men. I'm starting to prove I'm my father's son with the way I'm letting the business slip. Although, it doesn't help that I have no proof it was his men starting this shit.

"Of course I did. It's wrapped and labeled for the little man. It's in the back."

"Gracias. It's not like I've had time to go, and I sure as

hell didn't want Dove to see the present and ask questions."

"Do you think it's wise to keep this from her like a dirty little secret?" he questions. It's just the two of us because Marcelino's preparing the helicopter and Julian's got a stomach virus.

"It's for the best. If she knew the truth about my family, she'd believe I was like my father and find another way to escape." I need to get both areas of my life under control. It's time to take Julio by the balls and tear his budding empire to the ground.

I hate leaving Dove, and I loathe leaving someone else to watch over her while I work, but these things must be done. With the constant issues at the winery, vineyard, and the new property in Calabria, I've had so much on my plate that I've had little to no time to convince her that she should stay. Something feels wrong today. It's not just her anger. My gut is telling me that I shouldn't leave her there alone, but she doesn't want my mother to come over. She's pissed because I refuse to replace the tablet. I have, but it's locked up in my drawer. I want to give it to her, but there's a lack of trust that can't be worked out until we have time.

Soon I'll take her out, but I worry that she'll resent my lifestyle. She doesn't know about my siblings or the war I'm going through with one of them. I'd hate for her to believe I'm just like my father. There's still so much to prove to her. If only we had more time together and I spent it with my dick in my pants and my hands and mouth to myself, but she turns me into an animal. I always have to have her.

We're taking a helicopter out to visit my half sister and her little one for his birthday. I made a promise that I would, plus I'm supposed to pick up a special item I had her make for Dove. Her husband worked for me, but he died last year in an accident at one of the vineyards. He'd been drinking too much and fell off the side of a cliff driving home. It was devastating to my sister because he hadn't been alone. He was with his mistress, embarrassing her one more time.

"The copter will be ready to take off in ten minutes," Marcelino says. I nod and return to thoughts about my wife. She hates me, even if her body disagrees. Her body sings with rapture as I fill her with my seed, but there is no love. I live for her and don't know how to change her heart. She can't forgive me for the past, and maybe I can't forgive myself.

Fernando takes the present and a bottle of wine as a gift to our hostess and then we board the helicopter. I wonder if Dove has ever been on one. Will she be too afraid to go on one? Damn, I'm fucking obsessed with her. It's only a twenty-minute flight, but the entire time my thoughts are on seeing my sister quickly, giving my nephew his present, and getting back to Dove so I can show her I'm not a total bastard.

"Fernando, I hate to do this, but I want to make the trip a quick one. I can't leave Dove for a long time."

"She can't get out anyway. How about you send Hector over to check on her?"

"I don't want another man around her. One she can actually get along with. One who didn't treat her like a whore."

"Maybe a divorce is for the best."

"Heaven fucking help me. If you ever say that shit again, I'll forget we're friends. There will be no divorce."

My half sister comes running over. "You made it," she says, looking around. "I hoped you would have brought her."

"Where's the birthday boy?"

"He's coming." My nephew comes running, and I wrap him up in a hug and pick him up. "Happy Birthday, mijo!"

"I'm so happy you came."

"I'm sorry, buddy, but I can't stay."

"No?"

"Primo, come on—the pool's calling our name."

"Go have fun. We'll see each other soon."

"You promise?"

"Yes. Oh, and before I forget. Here's your present." He takes it from me as his cousins call out for him. Luisa has two siblings who have four kids each, all around his age.

"Thank you, Tio Victor." He wraps his arms around my waist and squeezes hard before running back to the house with his present.

"Luisa. Can you please get me that box?" I question and she nods, knowing what I'm talking about.

"It's already ready." She pulls it out of her pocket. I open the small box and examine the pieces.

"Your work is masterful." I slide on the one that belongs on my finger.

"Thank you." She blushes with happiness. Luisa's super talented and needs her own shop to sell jewelry. "It's just as you requested. I can't wait to meet her."

"Soon." I give her a hug. "I have to go and get this on her before she runs off."

We turn back and walk to the helipad. As soon as we're up in the air, Fernando says, "If you don't want her to run, you better get that ring on her finger and take time off to spend with her that doesn't include fucking her brains out. Take her on a vacation."

"How can I when everything is a mess? Julio picked a hell of a time to fuck with us. I should have put a bullet in his head all those years ago. His men know exactly where to attack without being seen." It strikes me that he must have someone working from the inside of my organization. "Son of a bitch."

"Someone's helping him, aren't they?"

"Yes, but who would be stupid enough to go against us, and why?"

"Let's think about it. There are about fifty men on your payroll from the vineyard through the family, and only a half-dozen women." So many of them wouldn't think twice of crossing me.

"Dove," I cry out.

"She can't."

"No." I whip out my phone and use her phone tracker. She's not in the fucking house.

"I'll call the security gate."

I try her phone, but she doesn't answer. "Let's get back now."

Fernando's on the phone and then hangs up. "Well?"

"Danny said when he got back to the security gate after a ten-minute bathroom break, Vicente wasn't there to switch off like he was supposed to and his car was gone."

I pull up the front door security and watch around that time, and there is my wife exiting the house, moving toward the back door of Vicente's car, but he opens the front door. Startled, she moves to it, but then he slides his hand on her waist. She freezes and gasps before getting in the car.

"He's a dead man."

"Yes, he is. I'm tracking his phone. He's at the market with her."

"Let's get there as fast as we can." I check the rounds in my gun, itching to put the entire magazine in his head. *Dove, what the fuck are you playing at?*

"Damn it. I knew she wanted to go out, but hell, why lie to me?"

"Because you'd say no. She's young, and you haven't given her a reason to stay."

"What the fuck? Aren't you supposed to be my right-hand man?"

"Yes, and I've seen you more than she has. She's lonely and bored. Vicente's closer to her age. Maybe…"

"Shut the fuck up."

"I'm not saying she wants him, but maybe she knew he'd understand and help her spend some time out. It could be innocent."

"You call this innocent?" I show the video of his hand on her, but what happens next tells me exactly his intentions for my wife. He adjusts himself and bites his lip before getting in the car.

"Shit, but she doesn't seem interested."

"Like you said, she's bored and, well, she hates me." It hits me that I left my wallet out. Shit. I open it, and my Amex is gone.

"Hey, bro. I thought you were at the party."

"I was, but Dove cut out. Can you track my Amex?"

"Yes. Give me one minute."

"It's last used at the market at the dress shop."

"She's out shopping." A sigh of relief hits me. She's not leaving. She's just sneaking out to spend my money. It's all my fault, but this isn't going to stop the spanking she's going to get. "I'm about twenty minutes from landing."

"Okay. I'm at the doctor with Mom. Do you want us to go to the house afterward?"

"Yes. I need to deal with this prick, and I can't just leave Dove home alone. We'll be back there in an hour."

I turn to Fernando and say, "Make the call." We're going to have Vicente pay for his betrayal. He knows I wouldn't have let her out in this dangerous climate. My enemies are everywhere, including in my home. She doesn't understand the danger she's really in.

The helicopter lands, and I summon two men to follow Fernando and me. They're to follow Vicente when he runs and bring him to the warehouse.

As the vehicle races to the market, my blood rages thinking about his hands on my wife. Worse, what if she enjoys his touch? We pull up to the curb and search for them. I spot her easily. He gets too close for my liking and hers it seems, as well. I see that nervous stance of hers and then I'm a foot from them when he does the unthinkable.

12

Dove

It's around two hours later when we sit down at a café. "How are you, little Dove?"

"Obviously I'm not enough." I shouldn't have said that. Vicente isn't my confidante. In fact, I get the feeling that he's escorting me because he's more than interested in just being kind. He's pushing my limits by calling me little Dove. I might hate Victor, but he's the only one to call me little Dove.

"If you were mine, I wouldn't let you out of my sight, and I'd always be all over you, sweet Dove."

"I'm fine. You don't have to cheer me up, but I told you about calling me that. He's crazy territorial over his property. I'm worried that he'd kill you for such familiarity." He reaches out and touches my hand. I stand up instantly and quickly step away from the table. I barely get three feet when he grabs my arm and spins me around into his chest and holds me firmly. "Let me go."

"You deserve someone like me." He bends his head to kiss me and my palm comes up to strike him. He doesn't retaliate because he's being yanked away from me by Fernando, and I'm being dragged backward by Victor. I can't see him with the way he's carrying me, but I know his touch, his scent. *Shit. I'm in trouble now.*

"That you are."

Shit. I said that out loud. He places me in the back of the SUV and then closes the door behind him. The doors lock and I watch him walk up to Vicente and punch him in the stomach and then in the jaw before coming back toward the SUV. Fernando unlocks it and Victor climbs inside. "Vámonos ala casa."

The partition comes up, and then I'm in Victor's lap. "My little Dove, we have a serious problem." His hand is on my throat and his other on my ass, holding me in place.

"What are you doing here, Victor? Don't you have your puta to see?" I spit out, feeling the ache in my chest expand.

"Ah, so you know some Spanish."

"Everyone learns the bad words first. What does it matter? I want to go home. I'd rather live with that piece-of-shit father than with you." *Crack*. He pops my ass hard with his hand.

He grabs my hair at the back of my head and tugs my face to meet his. "You're not fucking going anywhere. I don't have a mistress. I'm guessing that asshole told you that and you believed that fucker over me. It's obvious that little fuck wants what's mine. I'm going to kill him for touching you." He rips off my panties and then frees himself from his slacks. He barely tests my entrance when he buries his cock completely in me, sliding me down over him. "You are mine. You remember that. I already told you that I wouldn't betray you. That bastard almost has his lips on you."

"I tried to fight him off," I sob, my pain mixed with the pleasure of his hands on me.

"Yes, you did, but he wouldn't have had the chance if you'd stayed home like you were supposed to." He grabs my hand that I smacked Vicente with and kisses it gently. "You're my wife, Dove. That doesn't change no matter how much you want to leave me. Ay Dios mio. He made you believe his lies about me."

"It's not hard given our relationship."

"And yet you still didn't fall for his seduction. Why?"

"Am I supposed to fall for every guy that feeds me a line?" His hand comes down on my ass again and my pussy clenches around his shaft, loving the ire in his eyes.

"You will never fall for another. Do you understand?" He thrusts harder into me before his mouth crashes down on mine. Every pump of his hips up into mine drives his message home.

"Yes, Victor." I want to believe him. Even if he's faithful, I'm still just his fuck doll. He spanks me again.

"Are you going to come for your husband?"

"I don't think..."

"Don't think. Feel, Dove." I do, and I feel too much. He kisses me hard and then sucks on my nipple through my shirt. I come, clenching around him, and he floods my womb with a roar. "You're mine. No one is going to take you from me."

We slow down and pull into the estate. What's going to happen now? Am I back to my cage?

He helps me straighten my clothes and then tucks his still semi-hard cock back into his slacks. "Behave. I have some work to do to deal with this mess."

He opens the door and steps out, extending his hand. I take it because I don't want to push him any further. It's clear he has secrets that he doesn't want me to know about, but trust is a two-way street and both sides of the street are blocked by endless construction and wall-to-wall traffic. I don't think we'll ever get it clear, and it hurts to consider that.

"I'm tired. I'm going to lie down."

"Go ahead." He swats my ass as we enter the house.

"Oh my God. I'm so glad you're okay." My mother-in-law throws her arms around me. I know she means well and everything, but if she knew the truth, she'd hate me and want me far away from Victor.

"Behave, Dove," he whispers with a threatening tone only for my ears. He kisses my temple and then leaves.

"Come. I'll make you some tea. I'd like to talk to you. Don't worry." She leads me into the kitchen while Hector stays in the other room.

"Geraldo, can you heat us up some water for tea?"

"Yes, Dona Serrano." He nods and turns to the stove, preparing the water.

Once he sets the kettle on the burner, he brings out two cups and then begins to cut some lemons. "You're a saint," she says.

"Where's Maria?"

"She's working in the greenhouse. Things will work themselves out."

"Thank you."

"I'll leave you, but if you need anything, just hit the button." I've gotten used to paging them over the past month. Still, right now I don't want to get any of the staff in trouble.

"Actually, we're going to take the tea in the garden." It's October, but the weather's still great out.

"Then I will bring it to you."

"You don't have to do—" I throw my hand over my mouth and then run to the cabinet and pull out the trash can, releasing my lunch, heaving painfully.

"A wet towel," my mother-in-law calls out. Seconds later, I'm being walked to the table and helped into a chair.

"Thank you. I don't know what came over me."

"I have a feeling," Maria says, walking into the room, sharing a knowing look with my mother-in-law. "I think you need this." She hands me a small rectangular box. I'm afraid of the answer. If I am, will Victor believe it's his? He's been acting like an asshole for weeks after accusing me of trying to run away.

"Excuse me." I take the box and walk into the bathroom that's off the kitchen hallway. I turn the water on to trick myself into peeing and then open the box. Seconds later I'm able to pee on the stick. After washing up, I lift the little stick and the answer is clear as day. I'm pregnant.

It takes five minutes for me to work up the nerve to leave the bathroom. When I do, his mother pulls me into her arms. "Come have some tea. It's going to be okay. There's something I should share with you."

I nod and then we walk out to the garden where Geraldo has set up the tea. I see Hector standing around while playing on his phone. "Don't worry. He's just standing guard. Now—there's something I need to tell you about my past. No one talks about it because it's not good. My husband and I were an arranged marriage for rights to the vineyard. I was exchanged, traded, but it wasn't my husband's wish. He wanted a life that didn't include staying faithful, and he made sure I knew of all of his affairs. Victor and Hector have six half siblings. They hated what their father did to me and to them, parading women around the boys all the time. Victor promised that he wouldn't be like his father, but most of it he couldn't avoid. I know how you two met. I know that he bulldozed through your world and dragged you across the ocean to be his wife, but he's not his father. His motives are selfish, but they are done because he cares. You can leave, but I don't think that will stop Victor. He'll come looking for you across this earth."

She sees her son with rose-colored glasses as most mothers do, but he doesn't love me. I'm just a toy for him. I don't know if my heart can handle that.

13

Victor

I REGRET HAVING to leave again, but I won't have that prick try to steal my woman, and in public as well like he has no fear of me. If there weren't any children around, I would have put a bullet in his head on the spot. His disrespect that everyone in the market witnessed is beyond profoundly fucked up.

"Come on. Let's get this over with so I can come back and deal with my wife."

"The guys caught him before he pulled a mile down the road. Not a soul would blame you for that betrayal. His vehicle has been taken back and will be stripped after it's searched."

"I wonder if it's just my wife he was after, or if he's working for the other families. I'll get my answers one way or another."

He nods, turning into our own private road that leads to my meat processing warehouse. I haven't had to use it in over a year for anything other than livestock, but I suppose it could use a thorough wash and rinse.

Fernando waits in the truck, doing a check of the area while Juan and Marcelino follow me into the secured warehouse. Felipe is standing guard with Vicente tied to a chair waiting for his fate, which I promise is coming soon.

"Oh, what a big man. You had to use your men to get me. Too weak to do it yourself."

"You're a bold motherfucker, but why would I waste time dealing with you when I'd rather be balls deep in my wife?" He visibly angers, face red, jaw taut.

"You touched my wife," I snarl, snatching a handful of his hair and slamming his head backward with a forceful thud. The fact that he put his grimy fingers on my beloved queen pisses me off, and knowing that she would have been mauled by him if I didn't get there fast enough sends my blood boiling.

"She's not really your wife. She's your prisoner. She deserves a better man who won't treat her like a whore." This motherfucker has a death wish.

"And you think that's you?" I ask with a laugh, causing his face to sour. I let go roughly, making his head bounce. I want to rip the fucking thing right off, but I need more from him.

"Dove's better with me, and she was putty in my arms right now. She can't wait to escape your cage. You can kill me, but it doesn't change the truth. You treated her like a prostitute, and that is all you'll ever be to her. Her John."

"Don't talk about my wife like that." I nod, and my men untie him from the chair, but secure the rope tight against his wrists and hang the braided rope on a large meat hook and slowly begin to hoist him up.

"What are you going to do? I know you're going to enjoy torturing me. I'm counting on it because you'll never be worth her."

"Are you hoping that pissing me off enough will get me to end this faster? No. I want you to suffer. I want the streets to run red with your blood for touching my woman. She's my queen, and you fed her lies."

"It's pathetic how easy it was to pit you two against each other. All I had to do was type in a few key search words and you turned into a raving lunatic, trapping her, locking her up while you went to find out the mysterious *Firestarter*."

"It was you?" I make a mental note to have every single one of my men evaluated, phones pulled and given to my forensic tech guy.

"It's easy when no one's looking for me. Then all I had to do was treat my Dove with kindness. All it took was some sweet words and she willingly snuck out. I almost had her to myself. The only reason she didn't submit was because she was afraid that you'd kill her. Besides, everyone knows you're no better than your father. Soon she'll live in shame just like your mother." I punch him in the face, cracking his jaw. He laughs and spits, but it comes out as dribble.

"I've had enough." Pulling out my knife, I slit his wrists and then press the crane button, raising the hook that holds the rope he's tied to. Slowly he's lifted as blood runs down his arms and falls to the concrete slab.

"Let's see how long you take to fall or bleed out." I

wipe my hands and face off with a wet cloth. I turn to my guards on watch. "If he escapes, you die."

Fernando's waiting for me. "Where is Dove?"

"At the house with Hector and your mother. They are keeping her close." He gives me the camera to the house and she's sitting in the garden with them. The room is surrounded and well protected.

"While you were in there, I received a call from Benedetti's man Martin. He'd like to speak with you when you have time. He says it's important."

"Right now, I need to see Dove. Everything else can wait. In fact, set it up for around midnight when Dove will be sleeping."

"I will. Do you want me to listen in?"

"Yes."

As soon as we're at the house, I slink toward the back and send the guard away. I watch as they talk. Hector's standing guard at the other side while on his phone. He gives me a slight nod to let me know he's seen me. Good. I'm glad he's on his guard. "You can leave, but I don't think that will stop Victor. He'll come looking for you across this earth." My mother is sure the fuck right. There's no way in hell I'd let her get far.

"Of course, because of the baby. I don't know how you did it. I'm not that strong. I think it would be better to live without him..."

"I'm back." She gasps, looking up at me nervously. "Dove, come here." She shakes her head and sits still, looking scared. "Now."

She stands, coming to my side meekly. "Excuse us."

I grab her and cradle her in my arms, carrying her to

our bedroom. Once we're inside, I shut the door and lock it. "Sit."

She doesn't. "Damn it, sit the fuck down." She finally does with her lip trembling. Unable to handle the sadness that I caused her, I drop to my knees in front of her, my hands taking hers. "I'm not going to hurt you. I'm not going to fuck you. No. Not anymore. I'd rather never touch you again than for you to leave me, Dove. It would kill me. I know you hate me for forcing you that night, paying for your virginity, but I would gladly do it over and have walked out of there, guns blazing, dropping bodies if it meant that we could make this right between us. I'm not sure what to do to make it right. I look for the words, but I'm not sure that they'll ever be enough. I wish you wouldn't hate me for the rest of our lives."

"I don't hate you, Victor. I'm angry with you. Are you sleeping with anyone else?"

"I told you that I'm not. I have not been with anyone since before I went to college. It's been over ten years."

"That is hard to believe."

"It's the truth. Then I saw you, and you changed everything for me."

"I don't even think I hated you then. I was hurt, jealous, feeling confused because I was so grateful that you picked me. Then I was hurt that I was nothing but a convenient lay for you."

"Honey, you were anything but convenient. The thought of another man touching you was too much to bear. They had rules and warnings. I took you so no one else would. I pictured someone snatching you from me if I gave you an inch of space."

"But you left the room."

"To deal with Avanti. I'd been coming from his office, pissed about the entire purpose of the party, and then I saw you as I climbed the steps to my room. Afterward, I told him I was leaving and taking you with me. There was no way I was going to let you go. I wasn't gone long when I found you sleeping in my shirt. Selfishly, I married you before you could fight it."

"Why? So you know your babies are yours only?"

"No. Because I'm madly in love with you. I didn't know it right away, but by the time we landed in Madrid, I knew that this burning pain in my chest from the thought of you leaving was more than guilt. I love you, and I know that I don't deserve your love, but I'll forever promise to love you faithfully, Dove."

"I love you more than you know. I can't say exactly when, but it could have been from the first instant that you grabbed me away from that man with such anger. For so long I thought you hated me, but I felt the way you've held me close every night. It only made me long for more. I wanted the fairy tale. I wanted your passion as well as your heart."

"I was angry at first. I'd never paid to be with a woman. I abstained because my father made me sick with the way he let women ruin his life and ours. I took it out on you, wanting to punish you for making hunger for the forbidden."

"You have me, but you don't trust me enough to give me an inch of freedom. You keep me locked up, and then you're gone all the time. They told me about your father and all your other siblings, and I can't be your mother.

I'm not strong enough to watch you betray me over and over again."

"I'd never betray you. I could never enjoy seeing pain in your eyes."

I get off my knees and sit on the bed, pulling her onto my lap and twisting her head slightly so I can look into her gorgeous sad eyes. "I'd never betray you either. I hadn't expected for things to go as they had today. I thought I'd sneak out and come back and you'd be mad, but I never expected him to try anything inappropriate. Then he made the claims, accusing you of having a mistress. It was all I could do to keep myself together. My heart hurt, but I didn't want revenge. I wanted to stop caring about you and to be anywhere away from you."

"God, I hope the bastard's still alive."

"Wait, did you?" she asks with a gasp.

"Baby, I'm the head of my family. There's no way I could let that slide. Hell, even if I wasn't, that is unforgivable. He attempted to take you away from me. To seduce you," I snarl.

"You'd kill for me?"

"I told you I would. You're mine. I made sure of it that night. From that moment until forever. He noticed my neglect and took advantage of it. He'd been obsessed, aching to steal you from me."

"I didn't want him. I only want you. I love only you."

I pull out the box from my pocket. "Dove, I love you with every bit of me and I'm sorry that I didn't do it the right way, but I've had this made to show you how much you mean to me." I slide the diamond ring with platinum that matches mine onto her finger.

"You had this made for me?"

"That's part of the reason I left today. My half sister designs jewelry and I asked her to commission our rings, and it was her son's birthday. I went to see them and pick up our rings."

"They're beautiful. I love it. Goodness. I'm sorry I believed him for even a moment."

"Don't be. You wouldn't have if I didn't give you reason to buy his bullshit, but now that we have that settled, let's discuss what I overheard when I arrived. Is there something you have to tell me?"

"If I have to tell you then you're not a very smart man, but I will say it anyway. I found out we're having a baby. I'm pregnant."

"I love you. Shit. Are you okay? Was I too rough with you?"

"I'm fine. You weren't too rough at all. And by the way—if you think that I'm going to stand for that shit you said earlier, you have another thing coming."

"What did I say?"

"About not fucking me anymore. That masterful cock of yours is my favorite hobby."

"Good, because making you come is my favorite thing to do."

"Do you need to handle anything right now?"

"No, just your greedy pussy. I need a shower. How about you join me?"

"I was just going to suggest it. You have a little blood right here, and we didn't wash up after you fucked me hard."

"Damn it, wife. The first load is going down your throat."

"You bet." I carry her inside the bathroom and keep my promise, jetting into her mouth before drilling her with her back against the cold tiles.

We've just finished dinner when my phone rings. I look at the number and don't recognize it. "Serrano."

"Brother. It's good to hear your voice," Julio chuckles on the other end of the line. It's been six years since I heard from the bastard. He called two days after I took over to say he deserved a piece of the family inheritance. I laughed, and he hung up.

"Really?"

"Yes. You sound happy. Could it be that having a wife did you some good? A fine little thing she is too."

"Choose your words wisely, Julio."

"What? Are you that possessive of that sweet thing your man had his hands on?"

"My wife is off limits. I won't let it go this time. She's mine."

"I don't want a war, Victor. I wanted my share. I didn't ask to be born to that asshole. I just wanted my cut."

"You mean the cut of debt? Or the bodies of the men I lost fighting the Sicilians because he'd screwed us all?"

"I know that now. I learned what you did to turn it around. Besides, I've found my own little slice of heaven miles away. I'm calling you to set up a truce of sorts. With people snooping and asking questions with regards to my activities, I've been forced to deal with someone taking matters into his own hands. None of my men were instructed to take action on your lands. I might have resented what you had that I didn't, but I've got what I need and that's to wipe my hands clean of my mother's lover."

"We will never be close, Julio."

"I'm not asking for that. I'm keeping to my area and staying there. I just ask that you don't try to take it." I'm still going to dig into his story because I can't take his word after all these years.

"I've got no interest in your activities as long as they're not affecting mine."

"Good. So we understand each other."

"Take care, Julio." I end the call and feel a fuckton lighter. I already know who was fucking with my property. The tech sent me an email with a list of tower hits, which correspond to every one of the fires.

"What are you going to do about him?" Fernando asks.

I run my fingers through my hair, feeling the weight of the situation. "For now, just leave it. I know all the damn fires were started by one of my own, so until I have proof otherwise, I'm not interested in going to war. Have you gotten the report on the other men from Giuseppe yet?"

"No. He says it's going to take several days. It's not as fast as they make it look on television." I nod, suspecting that shit.

"Well, keep a lookout for any of our men who

suddenly disappear. I have a feeling that Vicente was just jealous, and my wife only amplified his envy."

"I agree, except I believe he truly was interested in stealing her away. There's something I don't want to show you, but it was on his phone."

"What?" He hands me the printed email from Giuseppe. It's a blurred-out image of my wife sleeping with a towel wrapped around her body. It's clear the towel slid slightly off, giving Vicente a peep at my wife's tits and the side of her ass.

"He's lucky he's fucking dead. I want that destroyed. Do you know when he took it?"

"Yes. The timestamp was the morning after we came back from America. We had to leave to deal with the fire and you went to get her the tablet."

"God, I feel like a prick. I accused her of trying to leave while allowing this fucker to creep on her. Shit."

"What?"

"She wasn't even safe in her own home, in her own bed. He would have done something."

"Don't go there. It's over, and he can't come after her again."

"From now on, not a single man is allowed upstairs in my home. No one except those who live in the house are allowed anywhere inside unless supervised by one of us."

"Understood. Are you going to tell her?"

"No. God, no. I don't want her to be scared to be in her home alone. I need to check on her. I'll be back for the call." I rush out of my office and upstairs, nearly colliding with my wife. "Baby, what are you doing up?"

"I was looking for you. You didn't tell me you were leaving."

"I'm sorry. I didn't want to wake you. I'm taking an important call in my office soon. Come, I'll walk you to bed. As soon as it's over, I'll come right to bed."

I take her hand and bring it to my lips. She's the best thing to ever happen to me, and I have a lot to make up for. As soon as we're in our bedroom, I help her back into bed.

"Victor, I might not want to know about your business, but I'm doing my best to trust you. I'm assuming because there was no guard outside my door that you're doing the same, or is it because you're too jealous to have someone watching me?"

"What? I never had someone watching you. Yes, there were guards outside the house who rarely came inside. Was Vicente outside your door?"

"How do you think I came to know Vicente?"

"Why didn't you tell me?"

"I thought it's what you expected. I told him to keep his distance on several occasions and he did for the most part, but at least once a day I nearly collided with him."

I cup her face, cradling her head, and breathe before I say what I have to say. "First. Let me tell you I'm sorry. I'm sorry I didn't believe you about trying to leave me and breaking your tablet. He searched those things on it while you slept." She gasps. "Second, I am a jealous, possessive, territorial bastard obsessed with you and wouldn't have put a man that close to you unless it was absolutely necessary, and never the same one. I'm sorry he played us both."

"I love you, Victor. I'm not going anywhere. Now, please go take your call so you can come back to me soon." Growling, I press her backward onto the bed and slam my mouth down on hers. I only sit back up after we're both breathless and disheveled.

"I love you madly." I stand up and adjust my throbbing cock. "I won't be long."

It's nearly midnight when I wait for the call that Fernando set up for me with Santino Benedetti. Once it rings, I put it on speaker since I want Fernando to hear everything.

"Serrano, this is Santino Benedetti. I'm glad that you found the time for us to speak. I trust the line is clear." I know it is on my end. My software makes sure there are no other listening devices or other interference that can intercept the call, but it doesn't mean I'm talking to the real Benedetti.

"How do I know it's you?" I hiss.

"You don't know that, but all I can give is my word."

"Says the man who betrayed his family." Like I'm one to talk, but I'm gauging his reaction.

A low rumble vibrates through the call. "Don't even fucking spout those fucking lies. My wife and my mother are my family, and I'd never do anything to betray them. Everyone else with the Marchetti name can go drop off the face of the earth as far as I'm concerned."

That reaction is more than genuine. I'd listened to an interview he gave to the press when everything went down, and it sounds like him. "Well, we have one thing in common. What is it that you wanted to discuss?"

"Avanti. I heard you were in town, doing business with him last month."

"We have unfinished business," I bite out. I've refused to take Avanti's calls after I returned. Fernando told him that I was no longer interested in doing business, but Avanti can't take no for an answer.

"Well, personally, I'd like to work with you and make you a better offer. I want the son of a bitch dead, but I'd rather not get my hands dirty. From the rumors around town, he's interested in getting your wife back."

"What the fuck? He's really asking for a bullet in the head."

"Well, then, we understand each other."

Apparently, I'm full of understanding today. I run my hands through my hair and think about my sweet Dove. "Very much. I wouldn't let anyone take my wife."

"I'm betting the way you rushed her out of the country and married, I doubt you'd let anyone come between you and yours."

"Damn right. So what are you thinking?"

"I'm thinking my wife has never been to Spain before and it's only fair that I take her before the baby comes and we head to Africa for business."

"That can work, although I must warn you that I don't tolerate anyone approaching my wife."

"I'll bring my men, but I'll keep them away from her. Trust me when I say that I understand. There are very few people I ever trust around my wife." After reading what I have on the man, I know he's serious.

"Good. When can I expect you?"

"In two days. I don't want to give them any notice that

I'm leaving. I have eyes all around including at that party, but I'm sure they have some as well."

"Let me know when you'll be expected, and I'll have cars ready to pick you up." I end the call and turn to Fernando, whose phone starts to ring.

"Hey, okay." He ends the call.

"Do you trust Benedetti?" he asks.

"Enough. After Avanti sold his wife to his brother, I'm betting he hates Avanti as much as I do."

"That's my take on the guy. I'll do some more digging, and speaking of digging—there's no need for digging with Vicente. That was Marcelino. They've managed to dispose of him without a trace." Marcelino needs a raise; that bastard has proven himself over and over the past few years.

"Thank you. Get some rest."

"I will. I can't wait to find someone to keep me up at night."

"You need to find someone special. It makes life a lot better. Goodnight." We walk out, and Fernando leaves. His house is located on the estate about a mile from here, and it's why he's quick to arrive at any given moment.

I return to our bedroom and climb into bed, pulling my sleepy, pregnant wife into my arms. "I missed you. Get some sleep, mi esposa."

"Goodnight, Victor." She snuggles into me with a sigh.

14

Victor

"Good morning, beautiful," I groan, feeling Dove's lips on my chest and moving lower.

"Good morning. How are you feeling?" She cups my stiff cock through my boxer briefs, stroking my meat.

"Wonderful." I look at her hand and see the ring. Fuck, it's perfectly shining as she pulls out my girth from my briefs. Her mouth comes over the head, and I jerk upward into a sitting position and press my hands onto the sheets to prevent myself from grabbing her hair and fucking her face. It's exquisite torture as she takes her time sliding her tongue from my balls to my shaft. "My Queen, mi reina, please."

"What do you want, my king? Do you want me to take it down deep?" she asks, looking up at me with her nightgown riding up and her ass completely bare.

"Yes. I want you to wrap those plump, fuckable lips around my cock and show me how good a wife you are." I reach over and spank her bottom. She sucks the head into her mouth, using her hand to stroke the rest of me. "You're such a good wife." I growl. I can't take it anymore. I lift her up and flip her onto her back, dropping down to her pussy and eating her sweet juices. Damn, she's delicious as fuck.

"Victor."

"Do you need more, mi reina?" I stare up at her just over her mound.

"Please," she moans, slamming her thighs against my head. I grip her calves and pull her legs apart and rise up until my weeping cock lines up with her heat.

"Dove, your pussy needs a thorough fucking, doesn't it?" I ask, skimming my hands up her body to cup her fat tits.

She nods, earning a tsk, tsk from me. "Yes, Victor, my king." A wave of lustful pride slams into my chest and I rock forward, burying my length deep inside her small frame. She wraps her legs around my waist as I fuck her. Our headboard bangs against the wall, and I don't give a fuck if anyone in the house can hear me possessing my wife. I take her mouth because every moan from her still belongs only to me.

"I'm going to come on your cock right now," Dove whimpers before her pussy seizes up on my shaft, creaming all down it. I lose the last vestiges of my control and drive hard until I pump every drop of cum into her depths. I've already knocked her up, but I can't help filling her womb.

Once we come down from our fantastic orgasms, I pull out of her and run to the shower, and then I come back and scoop her off the bed. "I want to spend the day with you, but not inside of you, Señora Serrano. I need to spoil my queen. How about a day of just you and me?"

"That would be great, but I promised your mother we would have dinner with her and Hector."

"Then we shall spend most of the day together."

I take her hand and lead her down to my office. "I know you've never really been in here, but I wanted to show you where I work when I'm home. Besides, I have a present for you."

"A present?"

"Yes. It's not even a present. It's more me making up for being a dick." I hand her a pretty pink gift bag with several things. She gasps when she sees the new tablet. "There's more."

She digs in there to find a credit card with her name on it. "What? I thought after I stole yours—" I press my fingers to her lips.

"You wouldn't have to have stolen mine if I'd trusted you enough to give you one to begin with. I should have given you that right away. I let my fear of losing you get the better of me."

"I appreciate this. I don't think I really have a need. A lot of what I bought was just to piss you off."

"Well, I want you to know that I'll still chase you down if you ever think of running."

"It's a good thing I don't actually run."

"What? I thought you ran." I do my best to glare at her.

"I was trying to make you feel bad."

"I think it's time for me to take you to see everything the estate has. It's yours, after all." We spend the rest of the day going around the house, out to the large gardens in our jeep to the stable full of horses.

"Ugh. I can't believe no one told me about the horses. I've always wanted to ride one, and now I'm pregnant," she whines with a pout that breaks my heart.

"How about we ride one together and I'll make sure you're safe?"

"Really?"

"Yes, and I'll teach you to ride once our little one comes."

"Thank you." Damn, I love seeing that light in her eyes.

"Saddle up my horse." Five minutes later, I introduce her to my horse, Raven, and then I lift her onto him before climbing on behind her. "Come on, boy. Lets take Mama for a ride." I cradle her belly with one hand and the reins with the other. Giving him a little heel tap, we take a slow pass around the estate. Dove tenses up, keeping her eyes shut tight. "Calm down, love. I'm not going to let you fall." I brush my lips against her hair, and then she finally settles.

"This is amazing, Victor."

"It really is." This feels so right that I don't want to take a moment to let her go, but I don't want to make her sick, so we return to the stables.

"Thank you. Today has been wonderful."

"Thank you for giving me another chance." I kiss her and pull away. "We have dinner plans and if I keep this up, we'll be late."

"If you keep it up, we'll be having dinner in bed." An hour later, we're arriving at my mother's house. Dinner turns out to be a feast and a pleasant evening. It's late when I finally carry my bride to bed.

The next day, I wait for their flight to land while doing my homework on my guest. From everything on the file and what I've learned, he's on the up and up, but it's all the things that aren't recorded that keep our worlds running. It's the reason we're not all incarcerated although he'd already been there, so I must be careful.

My phone pings, and I know it's my wife. I've only been gone for thirty minutes, but she was apprehensive about me meeting anyone from another crime family.

Dove: Please be safe. I smile, loving how good it feels knowing she cares. I've become a big pussy when it comes to Dove, but I'm not ashamed of that shit. Fernando lets out a chuckle after seeing my expression. I flip him off and then go back to texting my wife.

Me: Always. I must come back to my queen.

Dove: You better. I'm horny. Fuck me. She's learning how to get to me. I have to get my cock under control. I don't want to give Santino the wrong impression, especially when his wife is there.

Me: Good. I'm going to lick every drop of cum from your slit as you ride my face.

Dove: Speaking of cum. I can still taste you on my tongue. Can you get addicted? I think I am. Holy fuck, I'm in trouble. *She walked up to me in just her bra and panties in the closet as I started buttoning my shirt. She dropped to her knees and freed me, demanding to be fed. I came so hard and fast, dribbling my release over her lips and breasts. It was so damn sexy, I'm hard with just the image in my head.*

Me: Brat. I'll be back to feed your addiction later. Be good. I love you.

Dove: I love you too.

Smiling like a fool to myself, I love hearing her say she loves me. It's a feeling I'd never expected until I met her. Then I dreamed to hear the words from her lips, and now I crave them beyond belief.

"They're landing." Fernando says from the front seat. I have four armored vehicles with six men. As the plane comes to a stop, my team readies for a possible confrontation even if we're supposed to be on the same side. Exiting the plane a minute later are two large men in suits, scanning the area for snipers. Then out steps Santino Benedetti and a petite brunette at his side who must be his bride, Giada. The slight swell of her stomach and his hand resting lightly on it gives away her condition, which means his intentions are more than friendly.

"Bring the vehicle closer for Mrs. Benedetti, Fernando." I step out of my vehicle and nod as I make my way toward them.

"Hello, Mr. Serrano. I'm Santino, and this is my wife, Giada."

"Welcome to Spain, Santino, Mrs. Benedetti. I'm pleased to have you stay with us. My wife will be pleased to have another expecting woman around her." Fernando steps out and stands guard, watching Santino's guard. "I thought it best not to make you walk far."

"Thank you, Mr. Serrano."

"Call me Victor, please. I'd like you to ride with me." I point to the other vehicle nearest us. "One of your men can go in with my driver, Julian." Santino nods to one of them, who walks over to the other vehicle.

"Please climb in." They do while one of their guards hops in the front seat. My phone pings, and I check it out. "It's the wife. She's anxious for your arrival."

"I'm excited too. I've been talking Santino's ear off. I don't have a lot of female friends. One of them is his mother."

"Then you have something in common with my wife. She is with my mother most days, and they spend most days cooking."

"We have a lot more in common than that, I suppose. I was an Avanti," she confesses, as if I'm not already aware of that.

Santino growls, holding her close. "Not anymore, my love."

Santino looks over his wife to me and says, "My hatred for that man knows no bounds. I've already informed my wife that I want his head on a platter, and she has no problem with that other than she doesn't want me to get my hands dirty."

"So this is where I come in?" I chuckle. I suspected that was the case.

"Yes. Although I'd love to be involved as much as possible. I hate that bastard more than anyone. I'm sure there are others who'd love to see him being devoured by wild animals."

"We can make that happen. I'm all for making a body disappear."

"No offense, you two, but can you wait until I'm out of hearing distance? My stomach isn't the strongest right now, and even though he's a bastard and I hate him, he's the reason I was born. I don't want my baby's ears to hear about his terrible grandfather's demise."

"I'm sorry, my love."

"My apologies, Mrs. Benedetti."

"You guys can do all that manly bonding over bodies later while us girls chit chat and eat." She waves it off.

We both chuckle as she smiles, leaning on her husband's shoulder.

As soon as we enter the estate, Mrs. Benedetti gasps. "This place is beautiful."

"Thank you. It's been in my family for centuries, and of course it has a lot of modern updates."

The SUV comes to a stop, and Fernando and their guard get out at the same time and open the doors for us. I exit with Fernando and see my bride rushing toward me. "You're back."

"Be careful," I growl, wrapping her legs around my waist and giving her a big kiss. "I told you I would be."

"I was worried," she confesses, squeezing me tightly before I set her back on her feet.

"I'm here, mi amor, but let me introduce you to our guests. This is Santino and Giada Benedetti." I turn to my guests and add, "This beautiful woman is my queen, Dove Serrano."

"It's wonderful to have you with us. Please come in. It's about to rain." She brushes the hair out of her face. We lead them inside when Dove asks, "Is anyone hungry?"

"It seems I'm always hungry these days," Giada says.

"Let's decide what to make while the men talk shop." Dove pulls out of my grasp, but I drag her back for one more kiss. I'm not the only one with that idea. Santino pulls his wife into his arms just as I cup my wife's face. "God, I love you, Dove."

The ladies walk toward the kitchen, and I tell him, "Let's go to my office."

He nods but doesn't take his eyes off of his wife until they're out of sight. "Lead the way." Once we're inside, I offer a chair. "Would you like something to drink?"

"No, thank you." He adjusts his coat and sits down. "I'm ready to get this talk started."

"Good." I take a seat behind my desk. "So what are you thinking?"

"I want his head on a motherfucking salver. My wife suffered at the hands of my brother and his father because of Avanti. There are no words for the revenge I want to exact on them, but I'm not a mobster. I never set out to be one."

"That's fine, but how come you haven't had one of your buddies do the deed? I hear you have connections with the Russians and with the new Irish mob."

"Yeah. They would easily take out the trash, but Avanti has so many people in power around him. I thought he had you backing him, but my guy working the valet told me you might be the right person to speak with."

"He was right. Not only did he tell her she'd be dead if she didn't cooperate, Avanti's the one her father owed the money to. I paid five hundred thousand for my wife, and the bastard only needed fifty thousand. It's not that the money was spent for my wife—I would have given up everything I have for her—but not to that piece of shit."

"I want him to be destroyed, but I'd prefer if I was out of the country when it happened. I know you don't owe me anything, but I wanted to speak with you first about it."

"Do you have something in mind?"

"So we won't be taking too much of your time, my wife and I are scheduled to travel to my company's manufacturing facilities in Africa."

"Where? We have several from South Africa, Morocco, and Djibouti."

"We'll be busy, but I will say this. I'd wait before you strike on Avanti. I've heard some rumors, and there are other heads about to roll soon. I'd wait until next month. It's a short window to strike, but it's the best way to get to him."

"What do you mean?"

"I mean someone else is going to meet their fate, and you might catch yourself as a suspect if you head in too soon."

"Understood." We might be getting along, and I see

we could be good friends, but trust takes more than one or two conversations. What happens from now until Avanti's body is ice cold can determine our relationship. A minute later, I get a picture on my phone with Dove and a dollop of cream on her finger.

"They're having a good time."

"I'm glad. So instead of barging in on them, tell me about your vineyard. I heard it's expansive."

We spend the next hour shooting the shit about everything from the vineyard and his lumber exports while our women are building a bond filling the house with giggles. I have a feeling they're going out to the enclosed patio, which is just past my office. Their bond will solidify ours because neither of us want our wives upset, so we'll automatically play nice. Besides, Santino seems like a good guy.

15

Dove

"Oh my goodness. I love this kitchen."

"Giada, this is my chef, Geraldo. Geraldo, this is Mrs. Benedetti."

"Hello, ma'am. Are you ladies interested in some homemade whipped cream?"

I turn my head and look at him like he's crazy. "That's a stupid question." I swipe a large spoon and scoop out a bunch for Giada and then one for me.

"Oh, hell, this is so good. It's much better than the can."

"Thank you. Although I'm partial to the can. Do you want some strawberry tarts or apple pie?"

"Can we have both?" I ask while Giada rubs her hands together. She pulls out her phone and takes a picture of herself with the cream. "I want to tease the hubby."

"That sounds like a great idea," I agree, taking my phone out of my back pocket.

"Here, let me take it. I think since I met Santino, I fell in love with taking photos." She snaps a couple of shots of me licking whipped cream off my finger and I love most of them, but I send him the one that's the cutest and veiled in intent.

"Thanks. I'm asking for it."

"I bet. I just sent Santino one, and he's going to be all growly soon. He doesn't flip me over his shoulder anymore because he's worried about hurting the baby, but it doesn't stop him from scooping me up."

"Here you ladies are." I completely forgot that Geraldo's right there listening, and we both blush.

"Can we talk in private?" she whispers to me.

"Sure. Let's go into the enclosed patio, but let's take our goodies with us."

She turns to Geraldo. "Thank you for the treats."

"My pleasure." He's always proud to have people to praise his work. It's not often that he has anyone else to feed but Victor and me, so I'm expecting a masterpiece for dinner.

"We totally embarrassed him," I giggle as I lead the way past Victor's office.

"I'm so glad I didn't say what we did with the can," she says, snickering as I open the doors to my little paradise. Flowers hang from the wooden slatted roof, and in the center is a large patio set. The rain starts to fall onto the reinforced glass above us, creating our own little world of beauty.

"This is beautiful. I'm taking notes because Santino's ready to spoil me any way I want."

"Thank you. He looks like he's just as nuts as Victor."

"Totally as crazy. It's so nice to just be around a woman my own age."

"Me too." We take bites out of our desserts. We should have had a meal, but we can wait until later. "Would you like a water?"

"Sure." I walk to the cooler off in the corner and grab two waters.

After taking a drink, she asks, "So I wanted to ask how you met Victor."

"I don't know how much you know about your father's activities."

"Pretty much everything," she confesses, looking disheartened. I know her story. I remember hearing about it from my father as a warning of what Avanti was capable of.

"It was at the virgin sale party."

"Oh. Did he buy yours?" she asks, taking a bite of her pie as if it's not a big deal.

"Yes. I know it's terrible, but he saved me from one of the other slimy men." I don't want anyone thinking bad about Victor. I know his motives were genuine and loving, even if it took us forever to realize it.

She nods. "Your husband seems like Santino, obsessed with his wife."

"It took us a while to work it out. He thought I couldn't love him because of it, but in all honesty, I couldn't hate the man who saved me from something fucked up."

"Yes, Santino saved me, but I wasn't that lucky. It took a while and I lived in hell, but he took me and told me I was his. I welcomed his passion and love, even if it scared me." I take a bite of my food, feeling the weight of the conversation, remembering who I'm talking to. Giada suffered more than most at the hands of those close to her. At least my mother died and didn't sell me off.

I reach out and squeeze her hand. "I feel like we've lived similar lives."

She smiles. "We have. I'm so grateful that you were rescued. Now if my father was taken down, we could save others. I know that the other families don't deal in human trafficking or at least they're undercover about it, but my father flaunted his mistresses and the fact that he slept with many of the women that enter our home. Honestly, I'm happy Victor got you out because my father would have taken you after you'd serviced whoever bought you."

"Why do you say that?"

"He has a thing for blondes, gorgeous ones."

"What?" Victor snarls, causing us to jump and my fork to fall on the floor. He picks it up as he rushes to my side. He rubs my back and then kisses the crown of my head. "I'm sorry. I didn't mean to startle you ladies, but you said he's interested in my wife."

She frowns as Santino sits by her in another chair, taking her hand. "I don't know that for certain, but I know his past reputation. He always gives the ones he wants to bed a special piece of jewelry to wear with a tracker."

I look at Victor, and I can see the wheels in his head

turning. I most definitely received one of the special pieces. "What? Baby, where is that piece of jewelry?"

"I took it off in the shower that night. I left it in the bathroom."

"Shit. Fernando packed our belongings; if he saw it, he would have brought it." Victor calls his head of security on speaker while taking a seat next to me, rubbing my back. It's not just for me. I know he's finding comfort in touching me. The reality of the situation seems a lot darker knowing what we know now.

"Fernando, where is the necklace that Dove was wearing at the party?" he barks into the phone.

"It's in your suitcase in the small compartment at the top. I completely forgot about it, to be honest."

"Shit. I didn't bother to check for anything when I emptied it. It has a tracker in it. I want it destroyed. I'll bring it later for Luisa to deal with. No, wait. We'll put it on a plane to Mexico. Acapulco, to be exact, so they'll think I took Dove on a honeymoon there."

"Sounds good, Victor. I'm sorry I had no idea it had a tracker in it."

"Don't worry. Enjoy the rest of your day off. Thanks." He ends the call, and I'm curious who this Luisa is. I'm not going to ask because I'm already freaked out and jealous.

"Now we need to see if he sends anyone down that way."

"I can make a call and make it happen," Santino offers. "Johnny's a lot closer and has the connections."

"Thanks, Santino."

"We didn't mean to interrupt your little desserts, but we wanted to see if you ladies needed anything."

"I could use a nap," Giada says with a yawn that spreads to each one of us.

"Perhaps a nap is a good idea." Victor scoops me up and says, "Follow me."

I catch Santino picking up Giada as well. We giggle as they carry us to bed. Victor points to their bedroom. "Dinner will be at six."

"Thanks. See you then." He winks, and I know Giada could use some more whipped cream.

I giggle and then yawn as Victor takes us to our room. "It's time to rest, my wife."

"Sounds wonderful. Does that mean you'll lay with me?" I ask with doe eyes, pouting with my bottom lip out.

"After I eat your pussy until you fall asleep." I clench my thighs together, feeling like a cat getting her cream. The second he lays me on the bed, I know rest is the last thing I want.

I wake up and Victor's still asleep, so I decide to slip into the bathroom to wash up. We have company, so I can't forgo a shower. I take a long look at myself in the mirror and smile. My belly isn't showing yet, but I can see the glow of happiness. My ring shines in the reflection, reminding me that Victor truly loves me.

I turn on the shower and wait for it to warm as I pin up my hair. I'm only going for a quick wash. The water feels incredible as I step inside. Like a beacon summoning, I hear Victor get closer and make sure the loofah is super sudsy, allowing bubbles to cascade down my body, one leg bent while I arch my back and scrub my breasts.

The door's slightly ajar, and I see it move open even more. His eyes focus on me with fascination while I squish my breasts together, massaging them with the bubbles.

"Dove," he croaks out.

I turn my gaze to his, watching him admiring me and licking his lips like we didn't just fuck like bunnies an hour or so ago. "Enjoying the show?" I sass, parting my legs and running my soapy hands downward to my pussy, spreading my finger over the outside of my folds.

"Yes," he confidently says while unabashedly staring at my hard nipples.

"Why don't you come in and get a better look?"

"I'm glad you offered." He opens the glass door and joins me with his thick, long cock pointing upward and directly at me.

"Holy shit, the front row seating is the best." I take the body wash and squeeze some into my hand, soaping them up and then begin to stroke Victor's sexy appendage.

"Wife, you better be careful. You know I'm already close to exploding."

"I thought that's what you wanted," I moan, tugging on his girth while staring at his mouth.

"I want to bend you over and fuck you hard and fast." I grab the detachable head and spray his cock, rinsing off the soap. I turn around and bend over, spraying my pussy with the water. "Hold it there," he growls. I press one hand against the wall while holding the spray on my nub. Then he parts my thighs and slides into me from behind with one hand on my ponytail and the other on my breast.

"Fuck," I scream. The pleasure's intense and I let go, shaking as my orgasm pulses through me.

"That's it. Come so good, Dove." He grips my hips, pumping two more times before pulling out and coming on my ass. "You have no idea how hot that is," he growls, swatting my ass, and then helps me straighten up and takes the showerhead to wash off my backside.

"Damn, that was so freaking good." I'm still shaking.

"Take a seat." I sit on the shower bench to catch my breath. He washes up and then brings me close to kiss me and then turns off the shower. We dry off, and I check the clock.

"Oh no, we better hurry. We don't want to leave our guests waiting for us."

"Then you better get moving, mi amor."

Twenty minutes later, we step into the living room as our guests meet us there. "How are you feeling?" I ask Giada.

"Better. Rejuvenated." Her grin is so wide, it's obvious they were occupying their time well.

"I couldn't agree more."

"Ladies, would you like some juice or water?"

"Water," we both say. Victor walks to the bar and pulls out some waters from under the bar. He addresses Santino. "Hendricks?"

"That will hit the spot." He pours them each a glass

and then slides one to Santino. I take a sip of my water and see Victor stealing a glance at me and then winking.

Maria comes into the room and says, "Dinner is ready."

"Shall we?"

"I can never say no to food," Santino says before finishing his drink with a contented sigh and setting it down on the bar top. The men take our arms, wrapping them around theirs before leading us into the dining room.

Dinner's fantastic as always, but it's nice to have company, especially two people who understand our situation.

"So your mother doesn't live with you?" Giada asks Victor.

"No, she wanted her own place. It's been hard to let her go with the risks, but she'd been trapped so long," he says.

"She's around a lot, though. I know she can't wait to see her first grandbaby," I add.

"My mother can't wait either," Santino says, chuckling.

"It's so nice to have a little one to love and raise with the love we didn't get. I promise to make sure our baby never feels alone," Giada adds.

"You're going to be a wonderful mother, Giada." They share a brief kiss.

"Thank you, love." Victor reaches out to hold my hand and then brings it to his lips. I'm so glad that I've met them.

16

Victor

IT'S BEEN two weeks since Santino left, and just a week ago, his stepfather Rafael Marchetti disappeared. They fear that he's fled the country and won't face the charges against him, which there are many from what I read online, but I know better. Marchetti's dead. Santino didn't need to say anything else, and I'm grateful that he warned me against going to America again. Having the FBI on my tail for something I had nothing to do with would fuck up my business. I have my own bodies to deal with here, and our policia aren't interested in my activities.

It's early morning, but I'm sitting at my desk with Fernando, Julian, Marcelino, and Hector seated around me as we discuss business.

"So far everyone has come out clean. I hate challenging my men, but as you know, Vicente was in my home daily, attempting to seduce my wife, playing on her fear."

"We understand, Jefe."

"I'm grateful that everyone else is loyal."

"How are things at the restaurant, Hector?"

"All the numbers are improving. We've had an influx of tourists, so Lupe's pleased with the extra tours the winery has had."

"Good, good."

"Any news on the pendant?" Fernando asks.

"I'm waiting to hear back from the Irishman. He's the one who sent his man down to follow Avanti's guy." Just then, my phone rings.

"Speak of the devil and he shall appear. Any news?"

"Yes, big news. It seems Avanti didn't just send anyone. He sent your wife's father."

"Let's just say, a Mexican cartel learned of the thousand-dollar necklace that was accidentally shipped to the wrong location. It so happens that it was taken, and Falcone was killed in the process. I'm sorry to break the bad news."

"Yes. That's terrible news. I'll have to break it to my wife. She will be heartbroken." I smile as the words come from my lips.

"Thank you for letting me know."

"My pleasure."

I end the call and say, "Poor Dove has lost her father."

"What a pity," Julian says. "Couldn't have happened to a better man."

"Well, I suppose they may be contacting us soon for the funeral. If they can find us."

"I'm expecting a call from Avanti anytime soon."

My phone rings from a private number. "Serrano."

"You're a dead man."

"Avanti. Is there a reason that you're making such a very serious threat?"

"You stole my necklace and had her father killed for it."

"I did no such thing. My wife lost that piece-of-shit necklace."

"You set Falcone up."

"I didn't do shit. I don't even know what you're talking about."

"You're going to play dumb, but I know you found the tracker and planted it in Acapulco. That's why I sent that bastard there to get his daughter back."

"Planted it? Why would you put a tracker on my wife?"

"She's my whore. I want her back."

"You're a dead man."

"You can't touch me."

"I don't have to. Trust me when I say your days are already numbered. The day you disrespected me, forced my hand when it came to paying for my wife, you earned a death sentence. Now you have the nerve to speak of her like that, you're going to pay, and you don't even know when it will happen. Will it be in your food, medicine, your Viagra, or maybe in your liquor? Who knows, but I will relish the day you're dead."

"Bullshit. You're so fucking full of it. I'll show up and blow your fucking head off."

"Please do. You won't make it far."

"You stupid son of a bitch. I'm going to chop your balls off, rape your wife, and then give her to my men."

"Bye, bitch." I end the call because I don't need to hear his ranting and raving.

"Wow, you might just kill him by paranoia."

"Right? Make sure all flights coming into the country are monitored."

"You spot a single one of those American pieces of shit, you put a bullet in their heads."

"Understood."

We head out to inspect the cameras in the vineyards when my phone rings again. "Serrano."

"It's Vitali. I've just gotten an offer. A really fucking nice offer to take you out."

"Let me guess. Avanti."

"Yes. Tell me why I shouldn't take up his offer."

"Tell me why you would even call if you were really interested?"

"True. I don't like that scum, but he says you stole his daughter and we've seen the woman you're with."

"My wife isn't his daughter. He wants her to be his."

"Ah. Well, I must say he's a prick. I only called to let you know. I'm not interested. I made that clear before, but I'm not your only concern. It's strange that he'd offer a million-dollar hit on you."

"He can't do it if he's dead."

"Good. I enjoy your wine and restaurant too much. I'd deal with him sooner rather than later."

"Trust me. I'm not worried about Avanti."

"Thank you for the warning."

"Take care, Serrano."

"Same to you, Vitali."

"Well, boys, it seems that Avanti's trying to outsource

his killings." I look at my watch and laugh. "Excuse me, but I must break the news of her father's death to my wife."

I shake their hands as we stand. "Keep a look out. You know they're likely to use a drone to do their dirty work."

"We have control of the airspace around here, so don't worry. Any drone that approaches our area will be shot down."

"Good. Now, I'm going to comfort my devastated wife." When I get out of my office, I search out my wife. She's in the library reading on her tablet.

"What's up, Victor? I didn't expect to see you for a while."

"There's something I need to tell you."

"What?"

"Your father's dead."

"Good."

"Are you okay?"

"Yes. I'm fine. I'm more than fine. I know it's terrible of me to be happy, but I'm relieved. He's a total bastard. Who did he rip off, or was it your men?"

"He went to get the necklace. He ran into cartel men."

"Oh shit. Damn, that's bad luck." She has a smirk on her face, contradicting the sadness in her tone.

"Also, Avanti put out a hit on me."

"What?" she shouts. "You didn't think to tell me that first?"

"Well, it's okay. He's a fool to think he can get to me before I get to him. In fact, as we speak, the matter's being handled."

"I love you. Please don't die on me now." She sobs, pressing her head against my chest.

"I'm not going anywhere, mi reina. Give your king a kiss." She raises her lips to mine and I hold on tight to my queen, sliding my tongue into her mouth, tasting her sweetness. I pull back before I lose control and fuck her right here.

The sound of the helicopter landing brings a smile to my face. "Your guests have arrived," Fernando says. I enter the room to see Julio and his men.

"What are you doing here?"

"I've been offered a lot of money to bury you and he wants proof."

"Oh shit," Avanti says, "Not so tough talking now, are you?"

"Do you have my payment?"

"Of course," both Avanti and I say in unison.

"What the hell?" Avanti says.

"Did you think Julio needed to bring you all the way here just to kill me?"

"You fucking fool." My men snatch up Avanti and tie him to a chair.

"Julio, brother. I'm sorry I misjudged you."

"It's my fault." He gives me a hug. "This bastard thought I'd bite."

"Well, here's the fee for delivering him."

"Call it a wedding present. This one is on me. Better yet, give it to Luisa for her shop."

"She doesn't want assistance."

"We both have wives. Perhaps we need to order a lot of pieces."

"A smart idea."

"What the fuck is wrong with you two?"

"I'll shoot you if you don't shut the fuck up. My brother and I are talking."

"You told me that you were coming after my sister-in-law. Did you think I'd let you defile her?"

"The sick fuck told you what he wants to do to Dove?"

"Yes. If I were you…I'd take my time."

"I plan to do just that. Congrats on the new bride."

"Same to you," he says, pulling me in for another hug before leaving with his men. The men pull away, and I turn to Avanti. "It's so good you could make it." I punch him in his gut. He doubles over in the chair with a grunt.

"You piece of shit. All of this because I should have pounded Dove's cheeks. She's not worth it," he spits out, so I break his jaw in one smooth cross.

"She's worth everything to me. I thought you realized it, but I guess you've realized it too late. I've had months to decide what I want to do to you and now that I have you here, I'm not sure you're worth the trouble. You know what? I'll let you sit here and suffer." I walk out with my men and leave Avanti in the chair. I could string him up, but that would be no fun. Instead, I've slackened the rope on his wrists. Smiling, we all go to our vehicles. We drive back to my estate. I go inside and wash up and give Dove a kiss before excusing myself.

"He's on the move. Not very fast, but he's on the move." He's slack jawed and walking in patent leather shoes through the uneven hills. There's nowhere for him to go.

"Pick him up and promise to take care of him."

Hector laughs on the other end and then I hear him talk to Avanti. "Necesitas ayuda?" He's spitting but can't get any words out. "Let me help you," Hector offers.

He opens his vehicle and lets him climb in the back. "I'm Hector. Is your jaw broken?"

"Ssss," is all I can hear over the phone. He locks the doors after he gets in the driver's seat. "Hold on. I'm on the phone with my brother." He starts to drive and then says, "Victor, I've found this guy on the road with a fucked-up face."

"Really." I could just imagine Avanti's eyes widening as he groans and shouts, tugging on the door. I can hear Hector revving his engine, speeding up. "Are you okay?"

"He's trying to get out."

"Abra la puerta."

"Okay." He does, and there's a groan and grunt. "Oops, he fell out. I think I ran over his leg."

"I'll deal with it. You can go home now."

"Thanks. I don't want to ruin my driving record," he says with a chuckle.

I pull up seconds later to where Avanti lies in the road, bleeding and broken. "Did you think I'd let you get away that easily?" Avanti looks up at me with pure fear in his eyes. "Get him inside." My men come and pick the bastard up. We drive to the northwestern part of Spain into the middle of the wilderness. When we're out of sight, we locate a pack of Iberian wolves and dump a naked, almost completely dead Avanti in the middle of them. Driving away from the scene, we set up a spot and use binoculars to watch the wolves circle their prey. Slowly they work on tearing apart the old, sick bastard. His strangled cries can barely be heard as he dies.

"I guess he doesn't like being prey for a bunch of hungry wolves," I say, watching the wolves attack.

"I guess not," Fernando laughs. For the next two hours, we watch them pick the bones clean. Then we come and scare them away while we clean up the mess. Three hours later, we're on our way home with nothing but a small bag of bones left of Avanti. Once we're in our warehouse, he's wholly disposed of and the place is cleaned.

Now it's only a matter of time for hell to break loose in New York when no one can find the head of the Avanti family. Although none of that's my problem. At least I know he can't come after my wife again.

EPILOGUE

Dove

"Victor," I call out, but he doesn't answer. I know exactly where he is. For a super bad-ass crime boss, my husband is putty in the hands of our son. I open the nursery door and see Victor whispering to Alejandro. I stand there, leaning on the door frame with my arms crossed. I spent the day out with Luisa at her jewelry shop. Of course I had security with me the entire time, but they stayed a distance away.

After what happened with Vicente, they made sure never to touch me. Still, I behave so Victor doesn't have to make that kind of choice.

He looks up from our son and says, "There she is. My queen, your queen. The most beautiful woman in the world. She's back." Alejandro coos. He's almost three months old and a big boy both in length and width. I'm sure he'll take after his father. My heart's so full staring at my little family.

"My two favorite men. I've missed you both," I kiss Alejandro's cheek which makes him crack a smile.

"Did you have a good time?" Victor asks, drawing my attention back to him.

I nod with a huge smile. I'm so grateful that Luisa and I met and have become great sisters. Even his mother has grown to get along with her. We all know that it's not Luisa's fault, but the damage Victor's father did stuck with all the ladies involved. "I did. Luisa's new shop is so perfect, and she was swamped. By the time she closed up, I think she sold out of almost all the pieces on display."

"That's fantastic. I'm so proud of her. How many pieces did you buy?" he questions, lifting his brow because I don't have a limit on my cards and Victor lets me have whatever I want.

"Only one." He raises his brows, knowing that I have a thing for jewelry. I didn't know until he bought me a dozen pieces from Luisa. "Okay. She gave me two other pieces for free. She refused to take my money. I had to do it on the sneak tip."

"That woman. So, come here and give me a kiss," he growls sexily while raking his eyes over me.

I bend down and kiss his lips. "Let me take him now."

"He's ready for bed," he says, taking him over to his crib.

"I am, too," I yawn, having had a long day.

"Give him a kiss and get ready for bed. I'll be there in a minute," he commands. God, I love when he gets bossy. My pussy clenches. It doesn't matter how tired I am. That man does things to my body with his gruff tone.

"Are you sure?" I practically purr.

"Of course." I kiss our son on his forehead and then leave the room. I turn back to steal another glance of my men bonding. Smiling, I push off the wall and head to our room.

I open our bedroom door and turn on the lights. I'm shocked and let out a gasp. Our bed is covered in rose petals, and there's a bowl of strawberries in the center. He has done a lot of sweet stuff since we confessed our love for each other, but extra effort makes me so happy. I don't know how long I stand there, but the feel of Victor's arms sliding around me brings me back to reality. "Happy Birthday. I love you, Dove."

"My birthday's tomorrow," I remind him, leaning back into his embrace.

"I know, but it starts right now. You need to be pampered as much as possible."

"No wonder you were willing to let me out without a fuss."

"What can I say? I had to plan this special day." His mouth comes down on my shoulder, brushing my hair away as he moves up the column of my neck. "We have a big day tomorrow. Mostly you and me, but we can't leave our boy for long." He knows I hate to be away from Alejandro. Today had been the longest I'd been away. Three hours and even though I was having fun, I couldn't wait to get back to my husband and son.

"Is your mother gonna watch him?" I ask. There's not many people I trust with him. She's one of the few.

"Yes. My mother, Maria, Hector. Everyone wants to watch our baby. Now, I want you to relax. First, this." He takes a strawberry and brings it to my lips and I bite down on the sweet berry. I let out a moan which makes him groan. He steps away for a minute into the bathroom while I slide off my heels and start undressing for the night. "Now this way, mi reina." He leads me into the bathroom, taking my bowl of strawberries. The bathtub is filling with pink bubbles that smell delicious.

Slowly he helps remove my clothes, and then the water's ready. "Enjoy."

"Are you not coming in with me?"

"No. This is for you, but I must say, I don't want to walk away."

"Then you can keep me company and watch," I sass, hoping he'll make me pay for my smart mouth. He licks his lips and then rolls up his sleeves and takes off his watch. I know I'm in for it now.

I turn around in the bath, getting on all fours, pretending to reach for my favorite loofa and arch my ass. He doesn't disappoint. His hand comes down on my wet bottom. I cry out with the tiny sting and part my thighs a little. I'm about to reach for my pussy to play with it, but he stops me. "Hands up there. It's time for the king to take care of his queen." He pumps his fingers into my pussy from behind and it doesn't take long until I'm coming as water splashes all around me.

He spends the evening pampering me. First, a hot, scented bubble bath, followed by a full-body massage and two screaming orgasms just for me before he slid home, working on baby number two. After we settle down, he teasingly fed me strawberries and wine.

I can't believe how amazing my life has become, and I know it will only get better. I rest my head on his chest, listening to his heart race. "Thank you for saving me, my king."

"You saved me, my Dove."

Ten years

Victor

"Get in here now, Dove," I snarl, grabbing her wrist and dragging her into my office and slamming our door shut. Our men know to keep away when we're in our office together although that doesn't help much because I'll have her screaming my name loud enough to wake those we buried.

"What, Victor?" she huffs, doing her best to look innocent. She lost that little bit ten years ago and now my wife is all woman in every way. She can play coy, but it's just an act.

"What? What?" I look at her, raking my eyes up and down. She knows damn what. She's doing it to rile me up. After ten years she knows that I lose my shit when she's got my goods on display. We stand in my office and my wife is trying to go to a party in a tiny dress like the one she wore the night we met. This one is even more dangerous. Ten years and I'm a jealous son of a bitch. She's mine and I'll never get tired of letting everyone know.

"What the fuck do you call what you're wearing?"

"A dress. An LBD as a matter of fact. It's one of Luisa's." My half-sister went from making exclusive jewelry to high end dresses and she uses my wife as the body template. Fuck, I'm hard just looking at Dove.

Everything about her is beautiful, sexy and all fucking mine.

"An LBD?"

"A little black dress." she adds with a little more attitude that she's going to pay for later.

"Little is the operative word. You and Luisa are in trouble. Lift it up, show me what you have on under. You better have something under."

She slips her hands through her cleavage and pulls out a pair of black lace panties. "These?"

"That's not where they go, Dove."

"No, but I knew you'd rip them off me." She stuffs them in my mouth and then steps back, leaning against the door as she shimmies her dress up, revealing her tiny pink slit covered with a little dark blonde landing strip, and fuck I'm ready to land. I drop the panties and slip them into my pocket, shucking off my suit jacket.

"No gun?"

"Nope. I knew my wife would be causing trouble. Show me what I own, mi reina." Her slender fingers slide over her lips and parts her little pussy for me. "You need me to make you scream tonight don't you?"

"Yes," she moans, slipping her fingers into her sopping wet cunt and rubbing them violently.

"Give me," I demand. She pulls them out with a whimper and brings them to my mouth. "Someone's horny tonight." I suck her fingers clean and groaning as my cock jerks in my pants, straining the material dangerously. Fuck, my tailor's going to be paid more if I make these fuckers last. Dove's beautiful self always makes my cock hard.

"Looks like I'm not alone."

"Then turn around and bend over. Show me that ass of yours." She turns for me, rolling her hips backward with her ass popping out, round and plump. I watch the little show she puts on while dropping my pants and briefs down to my thighs. Stroking my cock with one hand, I slide my hand up her back, I press her down. Feeling greedy, I tease her clit with the tip until she's shaking. Leaning in, I grunt, "You ready?"

"Always." I line my cock up with her entrance and pound forward, plowing deep inside. "Fuck, you're so wet, Dove. You love making me jealous," I say as I grip her ponytail and then kiss her throat.

"I'm only for you. I can't help you're irrationally jealous." I slap her ass hard, watching it jiggle and turn pink. Over and over, I pop my hand on that smooth skin, grabbing both cheeks as I fuck her until legs give out and she comes all over my cock. I unleash every drop.

Pulling her upper body to mine, I grab Dove's throat and turn her head to get her profile and then bite on her ear before I confess, "It's never irrational because my fear of losing you is real. Always. You're the best thing to happen to me and I want you to remember that."

I'm in the middle of tucking myself back in my pants while she leans against the door breathing heavy, looking thoroughly fucked. I tuck my semi-hard cock down my leg so I don't give everyone a show.

Suddenly my phone rings in my pocket and I already know who it is before I pick it up.

Felipe speaks first. "Sir, the guests have started arriving."

"You've kept them away from my office?" I question. I don't want to have everyone hear my queen coming. Or at least not to hear all of it because she's gotten louder, freer and I eat it up every scream, making me harder.

"Of course. Happy Anniversary, sir." I end the call and tuck my phone away and then slide on my tux jacket.

"Our guests are waiting, my queen." I drop to my knees and then pull out her panties. She steps into them and I slowly slide them up her silky thighs until they're in place and then I pull her dress down. "Keep those legs closed. I want another son." I kiss her mouth. She clenches her thighs tight. The thought of carrying my baby turns her on as much as it does for me. "Good girl. Let's greet our guests."

We walk out and I lean in, "You look gorgeous, Mrs. Serrano."

"Thank you, Mr. Serrano. Oh and you're son's already growing inside me."

"What?"

"Yes. Happy anniversary." I stop and pin her to the wall.

"Damn, she must have told him," my mother says. I pull back, grateful that my jacket covers my cock.

"Was that before or after they celebrated?" Hector says.

"Mind your business. I'll take my wife where and when I want. Now enough of making my lovely bride blush. We have a party waiting for us." I take my wife's hand and lead her into the dining room and see the rest of our guests. Twenty family and friends. It couldn't be better.

"Long live the Serrano family." I rub my wife's flat belly.

"Serrano, Serrano," everyone cheers. Our four children come around to our side and hug us. Our favorite people are with us including our little ones.

"Serrano forever, Daddy," my oldest says. He shakes my hand and then hugs his mother like the good man he's becoming.

"Mommy's having another baby?"

"Yes, sweetheart," Dove tells our youngest son, Miguel. "Now let's sit down and eat. Mommy's hungry."

"That's because you worked up an appetite," Giada says. She and Santino made the trip with their children too. It's a fucking good life.

"I'm betting you did too."

"I do have another baby to feed." She winks at Dove. They almost seem to be pregnant at the same time. I'm just happy to see how close they are even thousands of miles apart.

"Thank you all for coming to celebrate this special occasion. Ten years ago, I met my queen, and stole her away from the world. Earning her love has been the joy of my life." I turn to her with my glass in hand. "I'll forever be trying to prove my worth to you, Dove."

Tears fill her eyes as I drop my head and kiss her lips. "I love you."

"I love you, Victor. Forever."

"Gross," my middle boy Jose says. He's a little brat, and I know he's going to be the one in trouble because he's always trying to test me, but I love the little man.

With a wink to him, I pull Dove in my arms and kiss

her harder and deeper. I'll always win that one. Everyone laughs and then I help Dove into her chair and take my seat next to her.

All the kids will be in bed after dinner, but we wanted to have them here to celebrate our happiness even if they don't understand the significance of this day. I want them to know that I'll always love their mother.

Throughout dinner, I steal glances at her and wonder how the fuck had I gotten so lucky. I had no idea what that day ten years ago would bring, but I never could have imagined it was the start of my empire. Nothing even compares to the family I've made with Dove.

THE END

Printed in Great Britain
by Amazon